"I want to make love to you," Mac said, the words coming unbidden before he could put a harness on his thoughts. "I want you. And if I'm not mistaken, it's only slightly more than you want me."

Toby got to her feet, and he could see she was trembling. "I think I'd better go now."

He headed her off at the door, blocking her exit. He undid the tie on his robe, then shrugged out of it and let it fall to the floor.... She looked terrified. But behind the terror there was something else, and he knew that something was desire.

"Please let me go," Toby whispered, but already his hands were under her wet shirt and covering her firm, round breasts. He felt all the fight go out of her as she leaned into him, her eyes turning shadowy....

ABOUT THE AUTHOR

Ever-popular Beverly Sommers is the author
of many published short stories, the most
recent a tongue-in-cheek spy series for a
syndicated newspaper chain. Born in
Evanston, Illinois, Beverly currently resides in
Manhattan, a backdrop that is often reflected
in her novels.

Books by Beverly Sommers

HARLEQUIN AMERICAN ROMANCES
11-CITY LIFE, CITY LOVE
26-UNSCHEDULED LOVE
62-VERDICT OF LOVE
69-THE LAST KEY

These books may be available at your local bookseller.

The
Last Key

BEVERLY SOMMERS

Harlequin Books

TORONTO • NEW YORK • LONDON
AMSTERDAM • PARIS • SYDNEY • HAMBURG
STOCKHOLM • ATHENS • TOKYO • MILAN

Published September 1984

ISBN 0-373-16069-0

Chapter One

She was an old deep-sea fishing boat, a fifty-footer in green and white, the name *Free Spirit* painted in red on her bow. She didn't look so much like a free spirit as an ancient spirit, the paintwork peeling from her sides in great strips. The wheel house was a good ten feet above the deck, and as the boat came around, she dipped from side to side as though slightly top-heavy. Scavenger seagulls followed in the wake of the boat, hoping to be thrown the unused bait.

Toby looked over at the Naval Air Station as she headed in toward Garrison Bight Marina. Two jets were streaking away from it; silver blurs against the clear blue sky. She reduced speed and took the boat in toward the crumbling stone jetty that formed the east side of the harbor. Something was out of place; not as it should be. Alert to even minor changes in her environment, Toby slowly surveyed the harbor until her eyes came to rest on the sleek pleasure yacht anchored in Captain Danner's berth. She looked an anomaly there amongst the fishing boats, like some rich man's plaything slumming. She felt an unreasonable desire to put a scratch in her perfect side as she cut the engines and steered in beside her. Toby didn't have much use for rich men or their playthings. Playboys, as she termed them all, did not appeal to her.

Rico had already dropped the anchor over the side and was securing the ropes as Toby went out on deck. In the well, three blue marlin and a couple of sailfish lay jumbled together, flies buzzing around their dead mouths in great clouds. The trip had hardly been worth the price of the gas, but the next day she had a client and the weekend was booked solid. These fish would be for Jay.

Rico was standing at the rail, his eyes devouring the lines of the boat moored beside them. "Ah, Toby—if we had one of those," he murmured. He had a familiar look in his dark eyes that bespoke of dreams.

"I'd like to know what she's doing in Danner's spot," said Toby, noticing the boat was out of Newport, Rhode Island. "Anyway, nobody would charter us if we sailed one like that; our customers like picturesque old fishing boats. Makes them feel authentic."

Rico turned to her with a grin. "If we had a boat like that, we wouldn't need to take out tourists. With a boat like that, we could go for the big time."

"Smuggling? Gun running? Just what do you have in mind, Rico?"

Rico shrugged. "Something more exciting."

Toby could remember when Rico had thought working for her was the most exciting thing that had ever happened to him. How quickly the young became jaded. "I don't think you'd find a jail cell exciting."

Rico reached into the back pocket of his shorts and took out his much-used comb. His dark curls looked charming, but he was always sure he could make them look even better. "You need me anymore, Toby?"

"No—run along. I'll see you in the morning."

"You want me to pick up the beer?" He said it casually, as though just trying to help her out, but she knew he'd use it as an excuse to buy liquor for himself, something she didn't wish to encourage.

"No, I'll get it. You could bring half a dozen Cuban rolls, though."

Toby could understand Rico's feelings. At fourteen she had longed for excitement, too. Now she took pleasure from that very lack of excitement in her life. A sense of danger was fun when it was an illusion; when it was real it managed to continuously unnerve.

She took out her knife and went over to the well, quickly cutting off the tails of the fish and tossing them to the waiting pelicans. The heads she put aside. She cleaned the catch, then wrapped the fillets in newspaper and put them in her canvas bag. She was just straightening up when a voice was heard from the yacht.

"Ahoy, *Free Spirit*, is the captain on board?"

Ahoy? The man was clearly used to yacht club talk. Toby tipped down the bill of her baseball cap to shade her eyes and glanced across to where a man was standing on the deck. From the look of the yacht she could have predicted what he'd look like—from the styled hair, aviator sunglasses, and Ralph Lauren sportswear, right down to the brand new deck shoes. His pants even had a crease in them.

"What do you want?" she asked him curtly.

He gave her a practiced smile, the kind that looks very authentic until you notice the eyes aren't smiling along with the mouth. "Is your dad around, honey?"

Toby made an effort to contain the anger she felt beginning to stir. She gave him a disparaging look before climbing the rusty iron ladder to the jetty. She found a hose, then climbed back on board and washed out the well before filling her water tank. Usually she had to wait her turn for the hose, but today she was the first boat in.

As she left the *Free Spirit* with the hose and her canvas satchel, Toby noticed the man leaving his yacht; so she moved fast and managed to be several yards ahead of him when she reached her bike. She unlocked it quickly, then pedaled away down Palm Avenue headed for the old part of town. She thought she heard him call after her, but she didn't look back; just increased her speed. Now that she was off the water the heat was powerful, and her clothes began to cling wetly to her body. Palm became Eaton and minutes later she turned left on Simonton. Soon after that she was parked in front of MerlInn and going through the gate that led into the yard and the entrance to the office of the guest house.

Jay was behind the counter and lifted his head off his folded arms when she entered. "How'd you do today?"

Toby went past him to put the fish in the refrigerator, leaving the fish heads out for the cats. Merlin the parrot the inn was named after greeted her raucously in indistinguishable sounds. "I just went out by myself. The weekend is booked, though."

"Yeah, we've only got about three rooms filled. You staying for dinner?" It was a rhetorical question as Jay knew she hated fish.

"I'll be back for cocktail hour," she told him, going outside and climbing the steps to the porch that ran the length of the front of the building. She unlocked the door to Number 7 and went inside, quickly opening the window and the louvers in the door and turning on the wooden ceiling fan, a device that did nothing more than blow the hot air around the room.

The room was almost completely taken up by a double bed with a headboard of light wood. It was made up with a brown bottom sheet, a pink flowered top sheet and two green-and-white checked pillowcases. There was a wardrobe with two drawers in the bottom, and a wicker chair. The room wasn't much, but it was a welcome change from her boat. She had a long-standing deal with Jay. In the summer she was given the use of the room; during the tourist season, which was late fall through the spring, she could use Jay's private bathroom to shower and wash her hair. In return, she provided Jay with fresh fish for his guests. Even in the summer, though, she generally wound up sleeping on the boat as it was usually fifteen degrees cooler than the room.

Toby stripped off her dirty clothes and put them in the laundry bag she kept at the bottom of the wardrobe. She was sweaty and smelled disagreeably of fish. On the boat she didn't mind the odor, but here, in the closed atmosphere, it became more noticeable. No wonder cats usually followed her down the street.

She went into the bathroom and examined herself in the mirror over the sink. The arrangement with Jay was a necessity, not so much for the bathing facilities as for the means of keeping her hair looking right. Her first glance at the baseball cap and the two pigtails made her smile. No wonder the man had taken her for a kid. From a distance she supposed the mistake was understandable. Only up close were the lines around her eyes apparent; lines due in part to age and in part to spending all her time in the sun. Her hair and skin were both dried out by the hot sun. She didn't mind her hair bleached, in fact it suited her purposes, but her skin had a deeper tan than she knew was good for it.

Toby removed the rubber bands from her pigtails and began examining the roots of her hair. They needed touching up again, so she got the bottle of hair dye from the bottom of the wardrobe and began carefully to paint in the dye from the roots to about half an inch out. She let the dye set while she shaved her legs and under her arms. Another necessity, not something she'd choose to do. She wasn't that hairy and a little fuzz on her legs and under her arms didn't really bother her.

Finally she got under the shower and washed her hair and her body, then dried off and rubbed lotion all over herself. She combed out her hair, not bothering to dry it. It would dry outside in the heat fast enough.

The clothes in her wardrobe were monotonous. Cut-off jeans and T-shirts for hot weather, long jeans and sweat shirts for when the weather occasionally turned cool. Two pairs of white sneakers, the use of which she rotated. The only other addition to her wardrobe was a yellow slicker that she kept on board the boat. She took pleasure in her spartan wardrobe. She could remember the days when built-in closets the length of her bedroom couldn't contain her extensive wardrobe. She didn't feel proud of those days. In a way, she didn't even feel connected to them. It was as though she were a completely different person now.

Toby dressed quickly and went back to the office. Inside was the safe where Jay let her keep an accordion pleated file folder. She assumed he thought she kept personal papers in it, but she didn't have any personal papers; in fact, she didn't have identification of any kind. She kept her money in it in lieu of a bank. She took out two twenties and a ten and put them into her pocket, then went outside and walked over one block to Duval; the main street of Oldtown.

Often she used Jay's kitchen to prepare dinner for herself, but tonight she was in the mood for a hamburger at Sloppy Joe's. She avoided the place during the height of the tourist season when everyone wanted to sit and drink in the bar made famous by Hemingway, but during the off season she was a regular. It had the added attraction of being one of the few places in town that didn't specialize in fish; this and a Mexican restaurant were her favorite places to eat.

It was early, only about five, and the place was uncrowded. Hank the bartender had her hamburger order in before she even sat down, and a beer appeared in front of her almost immediately. She limited herself to one bottle of beer with her meal. Any more than that and she developed a propensity for talk, something she couldn't afford. She needed her wits about her at all times, and for her, drinking was one sure way to lose them.

It was only a couple of minutes later that Hank put her burger in front of her; it didn't take long as she liked them rare. "How's business, Toby?"

She shrugged. "Not bad. How about you?"

"Quiet, but I like it that way. Made enough to retire yet?"

"What would I do if I retired, Hank? Sit around on the beach all day with the tourists?"

"We could always run off together to the Bahamas."

She reached for the bottle of catsup and poured a generous dollop on her hamburger. Hank didn't pursue the conversation; they'd been over the same ground before. When she first started frequenting the bar Hank had flirted with her as had some of the regular customers, but eventually they had all given up. At that time John had still been alive and she'd been living on the boat with him, under his protection. Even though his attitude toward her had always been fatherly, she thought the natives of the island assumed there was more between them than appeared on the surface, despite the great age difference. She and John had never disabused them of the notion, but they hadn't gone out of their way to encourage it, either. John had been as private a person as she was; not given to explaining his actions.

Since John's death more than a year ago, some of the island men who weren't gay or married had tried to come on to her, but Toby treated them with the same indifference as always, and they soon gave it up. She knew they thought she must be lonely, and most of the time she was. But there were worse things than loneliness and besides, she couldn't afford to get that close to someone. Being close meant confidences shared. She had no confidences she could share, and constant lying wore her down. And, if she had her choice, it wouldn't be a man she'd confide in anyway; it would be a woman. Someone like her. Someone who would understand.

His entrance into the bar shouldn't have surprised her. Sooner or later every tourist stopped by Sloppy Joe's, and he didn't appear to be an exception. He was coming in out of the bright sunlight and wouldn't see her until his eyes adjusted, which gave her the advantage. She was glad she had sat at the far end of the bar where the light was poor and he might not notice her.

She heard him order Perrier on the rocks with a twist of lime as he took a seat at the other end of the bar, then asked Hank if he knew where he could find Captain Tobias.

Hank motioned with his head toward Toby. "That's Toby down there."

Hank had said Toby, not Captain Tobias, but she knew the man would assume she was one and the same.

"Why aren't you called Toby?" she had asked him when they met.

"Because I prefer John."

"I'd rather be called Toby."
He'd laughed at that. "Then we'll call you Toby."
She liked that. She had needed a name.

The man was picking up his drink and heading in her direction, and she could see that he recognized her when he was about two feet away. He was dressed in different clothes, but still compliments of Ralph Lauren, and an expensive gold watch was on one wrist. The cost of his clothes and his watch was more than she made in a month. He did have class, though—he wasn't wearing gold chains around his neck.

After her cursory appraisal, she returned to her hamburger and finished it off. He stood silently, still looking at her, and she finally said, "Was there something you wanted?"

He seemed to relax then and took a seat on the barstool next to hers. "I annoyed you, didn't I? Was it the crack about your father?"

He had a slight accent that made him sound like a New Englander. She didn't bother to answer his question. If he had any sensitivity at all he'd know that it was. If he didn't, well, why bother trying to explain.

"Can I buy you another beer?"

He certainly didn't seem to mind being rebuffed. It sure wasn't her charm, which meant that he wanted something. "No thanks—one's my limit."

He took a drink of his fancy water while, at the same time, getting a good look at her over the top of his glass. "I figured Captain Tobias for a grizzled old guy—you know, everyone's idea of a sea captain."

Toby wondered if John would have taken kindly to being thusly described. He had been tall and spare with sea blue eyes and a cloud of white hair. Not grizzled in the least; in fact rather elegant. Not as elegant as this man sitting beside her, perhaps, but then John hadn't gone in for designer jeans or designer water.

The man began to look around the bar in seeming fascination. The ceiling was hung with parachutes, and most of the wall space was taken up with photos of Hemingway. Toby could remember being just as interested the first time she'd gone in there with John.

"I'm a writer," he finally said to her as though that explained everything.

"The island gets lots of writers," she said, finding it difficult not to say anything at all, and talk of writers was innocuous enough. And usually writers only wanted to talk about themselves, which made it safe.

"I'm no Hemingway or anything. I do travel articles mostly, but I'm also working on a book."

Why did he feel it necessary to explain himself to her? Just because his boat was docked next to hers? It certainly wasn't because she was the only woman in the bar. She might have been his type at one time, but no more; she wasn't even close to it any longer.

"Travel articles must pay a lot," she observed sarcastically, thinking about his expensive yacht. That boat cost more than she would make in her lifetime.

He didn't say anything in return which planted the first seed of suspicion. She knew for certain that the one thing writers liked talking about, above all else, was how much money they were paid for their work. Sometimes they thought it wasn't enough, occasionally they thought it was too much, but it was invariably their favorite kind of conversation. Anyway, he didn't look like a writer. The writers she'd met on the island cared as little about how they dressed as she did, and most of them didn't make enough for yachts, either, unless they were so successful she would have heard of them. Of course, it was possible she had heard of him; after all, she didn't know his name yet.

"I'm Toby," she said, hoping to elicit his name.

He smiled, obviously taking it as a sign of friendliness on her part. "Ian McQuade, but you can call me Mac."

No, she had never heard of him. And the name sounded as phony as the rest of him was beginning to appear. Something wasn't right, didn't quite fit. She had long practice in noticing those things.

She was also beginning to notice how good-looking he was. A full head of dark brown hair with glints in it that could be gray, but she couldn't be sure in the dimness of the bar. Dark eyes, prominent cheekbones, a straight nose and lips that were a thin hard line in repose. His slim body looked like it might be deceptively muscular, and his skin was nearly as tan as hers. There was something about a man that looked that good that she didn't quite trust. But then, there was something about every man she didn't quite trust.

"Look, couldn't I buy you a drink?"

She finished off the last of her beer, wiped her mouth with the back of her hand, then reached in her pocket for her money. "No thanks."

"I'm interested in doing some fishing while I'm down here. What I was wondering is whether you're available tomorrow."

"Hemingway never fished off my boat."

He gave a smile that almost seemed real. "If he had, I'd be pretty intimidated."

Toby relented. "It's a hundred bucks a day." She was in business, after all, and she could use the money. The upkeep alone on the boat took up most of the profit she made.

"Fine. Great. What time do we start out?"

She should have said a thousand. She had a feeling he wouldn't have blinked an eye; would have agreed to any amount she set. Maybe the other captains were all booked for tomorrow and she was his last resort. And maybe he was zeroing in on her for another reason entirely.

She stood up and put a ten on the bar, then turned to him while she waited for Hank to make her change. "At dawn, Mr. McQuade."

He held out his hand to her, and this time his smile never quite reached his eyes. "Terrific! Listen, call me Mac. The only time I'm called Mr. McQuade is on rejection letters."

She put her change in her pocket then took his hand briefly. It was hard, but not calloused like hers. It should have some callouses just from steering that boat of his. More if he ever did any fishing. "See you at dawn, Mac." She turned and headed toward the door, calling out a good-bye to Hank on the way.

Toby could hear Hank and Mac conferring as she left the bar. Well, if he was questioning Hank about her, he wouldn't get far. Hank was a gossip like all bartenders, but he didn't know enough about her to fill a paragraph. He was no doubt telling Mac that she had no interest in men, which might make things easier for her the next day. Although to be honest, his interest in her hadn't seemed personal.

Mac. If ever a name didn't suit a person, this was the one. Mac sounded like a friendly person, maybe a bartender, maybe a truck driver. It was certainly not suitable for an elegant dilettante who was doing the Key West scene. Now Ian; that suited him better. There was something sneaky about the name Ian that suited him. Toby was glad she had another customer booked for tomorrow. She wouldn't want to be alone with sneaky Ian even with Rico along for company. Anyway, she knew that Rico secretly aspired to Ralph Lauren clothes himself; he'd probably be Mac's fan from the moment they met.

On an impulse, she crossed the street and walked up a couple of blocks to the book store. She browsed a bit, finally settling on *How to Jump Your Way to Health*. A look inside at the pictures told her it didn't mean jumping off the side of a boat or the top of a building. It meant jumping rope, something she hadn't done since she was a kid. She thought she was healthy now, and she certainly didn't lack exercise, but she doted on "how to" books and this one somehow appealed to her.

Toby rarely read any fiction. She avoided anything with a hint of sex or romance in it. Spy stories made her nervous, and mysteries of any kind made her paranoid. She found that, in order to get any pleasure out of reading, she had to stick to nonfiction, and for the past year "how to" books had become her favorites.

The ones on "dressing for success" made her

laugh, ones on "asserting yourself" she took seriously, and ones on "home decorating" put her to sleep at night. Any books with exercises in them were the most fun. She'd tried them all, and jumping rope might be enjoyable to do on the deck of the *Free Spirit*.

When she paid the owner she asked whether he knew of a writer named Ian McQuade.

"Not off hand. Do you know what he's written?"

"Travel articles, I think."

"You could look him up in the library," he suggested.

She often wished she had a library card so she wouldn't have to keep on buying books. But library cards, like most other things, required identification. She went back to the inn and dropped off her book in her room, then rode her bike the few blocks to the library. She was glad to see it was open on Thursday nights, and went inside and used the *Reader's Guide to Periodicals* to look up Mr. Ian McQuade. She wasn't surprised to find no listing under his name. Whatever his game was, he probably hadn't expected her to look him up.

Toby wondered, though, about his reason for lying. It could be innocent enough. He could be just another rich playboy who thought it sounded better to be some kind of artist; maybe that kind of line worked better when it came to picking up women. Or he could be an aspiring writer, but the money for the boat would have had to come from something else. Maybe—a very big maybe—it was just a front, all lies to suit some purpose of his. And maybe she was as totally paranoid as she sometimes believed herself to be.

Jay was at the piano when she returned to MerlInn, playing and singing for the four lone guests who were drinking rum punch and eating the cheese and crackers spread out on low tables. Jay provided a European breakfast and a happy hour for his guests, all included in the low price of the room, and by the time they left for home they were usually all friends and vowing to return again. Jay, a frustrated composer, now had his wish; a captive audience for his songs.

The guests, all men, looked up at her entrance, but immediately lost interest and transferred their gazes back to Jay. Her landlord was a young thirty-four, had curly blond hair and a matching mustache, and the kind of muscular build the men seemed to go for. What the guests usually didn't know was that Jay had a long-time affiliation with one of the restaurant owners in town and very rarely strayed.

Toby sat down on one of the couches and helped herself to cheese and crackers. She could still remember the first time she had tried Jay's rum punch. It had tasted like Hawaiian Punch to her, and she didn't realize until she tried to stand up how potent it actually was. It had been the only time in recent years she had done an inordinate amount of talking. Now she stuck to beer.

Even in the large room with cross ventilation and all the fans going the evening was hot, and Toby was sure she'd end up sleeping on the deck of her boat.

When happy hour ended, the men headed for the bars on Duval Street and Toby helped Jay clean up.

"The fish were great," he told her.

"Glad you liked them."

"I tried to promote your charter boat to the guys, but when they found out you went out at dawn they nearly fainted. That's about the time they expect to get in, I guess."

"I'm booked up for tomorrow anyway, but thanks."

When the sun began to set, she said goodnight to Jay and retrieved her baseball cap and book from her room. She stopped in La Bodega down the street for a couple of six packs of beer, then, feeling generous, added a couple of bottles of Perrier. She thought the price for water was outrageous.

An orange ball of fire was sinking past the horizon as she rode by the victorian houses on her right, and the water on her left. Other cyclists were out, but despite the signs around town suggesting that visitors rent bikes and keep the cars out of the crowded streets, groups of rowdy college students were cruising in their cars, causing traffic congestion at every corner.

The architecture of the houses was one of the things Toby liked best about Key West. In California the houses had mostly been new and made of stucco. Here they were all old and made of wood, from the small conch houses to the larger Victorian structures with their turrets and gables. One of her favorites was called The Artist House and was painted in shades of violet with deep purple shutters. Toby sometimes wondered what it would be like to own one of the small conch houses, but knew that buildings tended to make her feel closed-in. Only on the boat did she feel truly free.

She noticed the yacht was dark when she boarded her own boat. The nigmatic Mr. McQuade must still be in town. Maybe she'd get lucky, and he'd stay out so late he wouldn't wake up in time in the morning. But somehow she didn't think that would be the case.

She put the beer and Perrier in the small refrigerator in the galley, then stretched out on her bunk in the cabin to look at her new book. What she found out was that jumping rope was good for the cardiovascular system. She no longer smoked, she wasn't overweight, and she figured her heart should be in pretty good shape. On the other hand, the book mentioned tension and stress, and she'd had her share of that the last few years. She might give it a try; she had plenty of rope around the boat, but not tonight. Tonight she needed plenty of sleep to be alert with Mr. McQuade the following day.

Toby put aside the book and got out her bottle of mosquito repellent, putting liberal doses of it on her arms and legs and face. This also dried out her skin, but she found dry skin preferable to being covered with bites. Leaving just her shoes below, she padded barefoot up to the deck and spread out her sleeping bag.

On her back, her eyes to the sky, she noticed something she hadn't noticed before. The sky was fast becoming overcast, and it looked like it would storm before morning. She didn't care—it was cooler on deck, and the first drops of rain would wake her so that she could move down to the cabin. And a good rain should relieve some of the humidity in the air.

She just hoped it wouldn't be a night for dreams. Some people had nightmares about hell, some about the war. She had nightmares about California. One day she hoped they'd cease.

Chapter Two

They'd been hearing about a Key West connection for some time. But Key West wasn't Miami where a couple of hundred agents could get lost in the crowd. It was a small, closely-knit community where most of the tourists, by lieu of being college students or homosexuals, stood out from the regular islanders in various ways. But there were others, notably the sports fisherman who knew the best deep-sea fishing was in the gulf stream, and it was decided this would be the best cover. The writers who seemed to be drawn to the island were also mentioned, and so it was decided, in some higher up's wisdom, that he should pose as a combination of the two. Since Mac had done little fishing of any kind, he would enter as a combination rich man/fledgling writer-of-travel-articles, with a yen to try his hand at fishing. The "rich man" part was deemed a necessity as he would need the high-powered motor craft if he was to intercept the large shipment thought to be coming in to Key West.

It was known that the shipment would be coming from the Bahamas; it was suspected the transfer would take place by means of fishing boats rendez-vousing in the waters. An immediate investigation was launched with regard to the captains of charter boats. One, a Captain Danner, was cleared of all suspicion early on. It was learned from the island police, and substantiated by hospital records, that the captain's son had died of an overdose of drugs and, as a result, the captain was fanatical in his hatred of anybody connected to drugs in any way. He even refused to accept the government's offer to reimburse him for time lost when his mooring was taken up by their agent; instead he set up business on Key Largo for the duration of the investigation.

Some irregularities were found in the investigations of the other captains, but none looked so suspect to the investigating team as those of a certain Captain Tobias. In a search for bank accounts, IRS returns or records of any kind, Captain Tobias seemed not to exist. Anyone seeming not to exist was someone the government wanted to investigate in any case.

Alastair McTaggert, called Mac since he was old enough to volubly protest his given name, had headed the investigation from the start. When it was agreed that, with a properly styled haircut and the right clothes, he could pass for a man of leisure as well as any and better than most, Mac had been given a crash course in navigation and sent to do the job.

Into the necessarily luxuriously furnished state-room, he had brought the tools of his supposed trade: a portable typewriter, which he was able to use slowly with two fingers; a dictionary; *Roget's Thesaurus*, and a large map of the world, which he tacked to the paneled wall. He filled the built-in bookcase with travel books and spread a few travel magazines around on the coffee table. He hadn't had time to actually read any of this deceptive literature, but he'd been around a little and figured he could fake travel stories if the subject ever came up. And he was *very* familiar with certain South American countries whose interests paralleled those of his agency.

Mac navigated his boat into Garrison Bight in the middle of the day at a time when the charter fishing boats would all be at sea. It had been an easy sail down from Miami with good weather all the way, although storms were expected by the weekend. Once docked, he retired to his cabin to change into his new finery. He should have broken in the clothes while in Miami, but had hesitated to have his friends see him in the kind of ridiculous attire he scorned.

Looking at himself now in the full-length mirror attached to his wardrobe door, he shook his head in amusement at his unfamiliar image. It was usually required that he look either a criminal type or like someone of the drug culture. On his own time he preferred well-worn jeans and a T-shirt. Now he looked like he might have looked if he'd used his law degree to enter his father's Boston law firm, which only confirmed for him that his career choice had been the right one. Financial success was fine, but he preferred adventure. And he also preferred not to walk around looking like Madison Avenue's idea of a male model.

The gold watch was his own, a gift from one of his ex-wives in appreciation of all the alimony the court had awarded her; the haircut was compliments of

Adolpho of Miami Beach, an experience he wouldn't soon forget; and his clothes were left to the judgment of an enthusiastic salesman in the Polo Shop of the Bal Harbour Shopping Mall in Miami Beach. All together they gave Mac the kind of appearance he was going to be embarrassed to be seen sporting in public. He only hoped the gay population of Key West could control themselves when he appeared in their midst.

He was trying to decide whether he had time to walk into town and look around when the *Free Spirit* docked earlier than he had anticipated and he watched from the window as a youth, who appeared to be Cuban, dropped the anchor and secured the ropes. He was soon joined by a young girl, a pre-teen judging from her hairdo, a precocious pre-teen judging by her body. When the youth left the boat and there was still no sign of Captain Tobias, Mac went up on deck to see if he could determine his whereabouts. He thought it would be perfectly normal behavior on his part, or rather the part he was playing, to engage the captain for the purpose of some fishing the following day. Whenever possible, Mac liked to get the feel of an adversary, and if he could actually talk to him, see him at close quarters, it was a distinct advantage.

The girl was now kneeling down on the deck, her hat blocking most of her face, and he called out, "Ahoy," and inquired whether the captain was around. His paternal grandfather had raced yachts during the summer, often taking Mac with him when he was a boy, and he seemed to remember one yelled *ahoy* instead of just saying something normal like *hi* or *hello*. He felt as silly yelling *ahoy* as he felt wearing his new clothes. Not that it mattered though—the kid wouldn't know what he was wearing.

Without appearing to even look up, she asked him what he wanted in a surly tone of voice, a voice somewhat intriguing as it sounded like the voice of a young boy rather than a girl. The voice would be cute in a boy, the hoarseness appealing; in a girl it sounded provocative.

"You're getting to be a dirty old man, Mac," he warned himself. *First you notice the kid's body, now you're intrigued by her voice.*

He gave her what he hoped was an avuncular smile and asked her if her dad was around. He assumed she was Captain Tobias's daughter, or maybe even granddaughter, as she didn't look old enough to be working for a living.

She totally ignored him this time, and he began to feel uncomfortable. Maybe she thought he was coming on to her and would tell her father, and that was about the last thing he wanted. He had to get off on the right foot with the captain, and being thought to have flirted with his nubile young daughter certainly wouldn't be the right way.

Mac waited, thinking the captain would appear eventually, but when he didn't and the girl went off the boat and walked away, he got off too, thinking he'd ask her again about her father's whereabouts. She seemed to sense he was following her and he watched as she hurriedly unlocked her bike and began to ride away. He decided not to even call after her. Better to back off at this point than to frighten her and, in the doing, antagonize her father.

Anyway, maybe the captain wasn't around for some reason. Maybe the two kids had taken the boat out by themselves. He certainly didn't want to get the instant reputation of being a lecherous old man by following some young girl. Maybe *he* knew he didn't go for young girls, but strangers didn't know his sexual preferences. Which, as a matter of fact, were quite normal, he thought. He liked mature women, preferably dark and volatile; ones whose experience and appetites matched his own. Maria, his current lady friend back in Miami, met his requirements. Although lately even Maria was showing signs of wanting to settle down, which rang her death knell as far as he was concerned. He'd already tried settling down twice and he didn't believe in the old axiom about three being a charm. One hadn't been a charm, the second had been worse, and as far as he was concerned three would be disastrous.

It was early for dinner, but he'd missed lunch, so he decided to walk into town and treat himself to a lobster dinner. After all—his expenses were being paid, and if he couldn't find a place with good lobster, he'd settle for a thick steak.

He headed in the direction the girl had taken and admired the prettiness of the town along the way. It looked at least a hundred years older than Miami, but then he guessed it probably was. He didn't like small towns himself, couldn't stand the peace and quiet, but he could see it would have been a nice place to grow up. And he sure couldn't complain about the weather. It was hot and humid, but not nearly as hot and humid as Miami, and anyway he liked hot and humid.

Cold New England winters weren't something he ever missed. Neither were cold New Englanders, for that matter. His first wife had been one of those.

Mac found a restaurant on Duval called The Fountains where he could eat outdoors, and took a seat at one of the tables. Except for a couple of people having drinks, he was the only one there. A bright-eyed waiter came over with a menu and asked him if he wanted a drink. He wanted a drink, in fact, he'd like several of them, but he shook his head no. First there was the matter of the little drinking problem he acquired while married to his second wife. Although he wouldn't exactly call it acquired: more like forced on him by the circumstances. And then there was the rule that you didn't drink while on the job unless required to. He knew he could hold his liquor, but even the best drinkers sometimes said too much while under the influence.

When the waiter came back, he ordered lobster and a baked potato with sour cream and chives, and Russian dressing on his salad. And a Perrier on the rocks with a lime twist. Mac almost laughed out loud when he ordered it, thinking it damn well went with the way he was dressed. He could wait. He'd belt a couple down when he was alone in his cabin later before going to bed. He had brought along a couple of bottles for just such a contingency.

It wasn't Maine lobster but it wasn't bad, and when he was finished with everything he was still hungry and ordered a slice of the famous Key Lime pie. Which didn't turn out to be as good as it sounded, but he ate it all anyway. The waiter brought coffee and he drank it black while deciding what to do next. Maybe he'd hit a few bars, inquire as to the whereabouts of the elusive Captain Tobias. And if that didn't turn up any results, he'd go back to his boat and wait it out.

He knew as soon as he was two feet inside the first bar that it was a gay bar, but an ironic thing happened. He looked so much like what the stereotypical gay looked like—with his styled hair and designer clothes—that the guys in the bar didn't think he possibly could be and they ignored him after a first look. He turned right around and went back outside. Next he tried Rick's, which turned out to be a college hangout and not the kind of place he expected a bunch of fishermen to hang out. Just for the hell of it he drank a fast shot of Scotch, then left in a hurry before he could be tempted to have another.

Across the street was Sloppy Joe's, and he thought he'd try that one and then get off Duval Street where probably only the tourists hung out, anyway. The sea captains probably knew likelier bars.

The bar was dark and almost empty, and he ordered another Perrier, then asked the bartender if he knew where to find Captain Tobias. "That's Toby down there," the bartender told him, motioning with his head to the other end of the bar.

Mac's eyes were beginning to adjust to the darkness in the bar and he could tell it was a female, but he was halfway down the length of the bar before he recognized her for the girl on the boat. Only he was fast revising the *girl* to read *woman*.

She seemed to be looking him over. He felt plain ridiculous in his fancy clothes and holding the glass of fancy water. He saw she was having a beer and he kept revising her age upward. It was pretty dim in the bar, but he figured she had to be at least college age.

She was dressed the same, but this time wasn't wearing her baseball hat, and her blonde shoulder-length hair and straight bangs were catching all the available light in the bar. He caught a glimpse of dark eyes, but couldn't tell whether they were brown or a deep blue, and then she turned away from him and finished eating a hamburger that was set before her. While she was busy eating he sneaked a look at her body. It wasn't the Playboy bunny kind of shape that he generally favored, but still and all he thought she had a lot more than warranted her going around without a bra, which was clearly the case. Her legs were smooth and finely muscled. No, no Playboy bunny, but he wouldn't throw her out of bed, either.

She finally finished eating, wiped off her mouth with a napkin, then shot him an annoyed look. "Was there something you wanted?" she asked, and he got the idea she thought he was trying to pick her up.

Well, she could think again. The last time Mac had tried to pick up someone who looked like her had been back in college when all the girls had looked like her. These days he liked his women in tight, low-cut dresses and heels so high they could barely walk. And any woman who looked like she could jog even a block was not for him. But the voice was great. Low and hoarse and sexy as hell. Now if the rest of her matched the voice....

She was probably one of those militant feminists, he mused. She had gotten annoyed when he asked about her father earlier. Well, if she were captain of her own boat, he guessed he couldn't blame her. And since it was imperative now that he get on her good side, he said, "I annoyed you, didn't I? Was it the crack about your father?"

That was probably the best attempt at an apology Mac had ever made to a woman, but it seemed to have no effect on her at all. She ignored him, looking instead across the bar as though she were fascinated by the display of bottles. Maybe it was a hint. She might be expecting him to buy her a drink. And why not? A few drinks might loosen the iron maiden up.

"Can I buy you another beer?" He gave her his best smile, but she didn't even look in his direction. He better start explaining himself or she sure would begin to think it was a pick-up attempt.

She finally said, "No thanks—one's my limit."

One beer was her *limit*? What happened when she had two, did she suddenly get friendly? He decided to joke with her a little; tell her she wasn't his idea of what a sea captain looked like, but she continued to ignore him. Maybe he should just tell her that college girls didn't appeal to him and he had a real woman back in Miami. On second thought, maybe he shouldn't.

Now that his eyes had adjusted, he began to see that the walls of the bar were covered with pictures of Hemingway. Which reminded him in a hurry that he was supposed to be a writer.

"I'm a writer," he told her, figuring that for a good opening. He was sure a young girl would find a writer fascinating. But all she did was tell him that the island got lots of writers as though it were no big deal.

He waited for her to ask him what he wrote, but he waited in vain. She was sure the most close-mouthed female he had ever come across. Then it struck him that she seemed not to mind not knowing what she didn't already know, and that maybe her not asking questions meant she didn't want questions asked of her in return. Which made two of them, as a matter of fact.

But writers probably talked a lot, and he better get somewhat in character. So Mac told her he wrote travel articles, and when that didn't elicit any response, followed it up by telling her he was working on a book. Which wasn't the smartest thing in the world to say because if she now asked him what the book was about he wouldn't have a clue. An exposé on drug smuggling? No, he couldn't say that. He could sure write one, though.

She made some kind of sarcastic remark about travel articles paying well, and that shut him up. First of all, he hadn't a clue what travel articles paid, and second of all, he was fairly certain whatever it paid it wouldn't begin to pay for his yacht. He supposed that now was the time to infer that he was also a rich playboy type, but if she couldn't tell that already from his clothes he was out of luck. He didn't suppose real playboys had to point out what they were.

Then she surprised the hell out of him by saying, "I'm Toby," the first friendly thing she had said so far. He was so relieved that he smiled at her and gave her his phony name, but then, when she didn't say anything else, he asked her again if he could buy her another drink.

She said no, then started to pay for her burger and beer, and he knew he had to move fast. So he told her he was interested in chartering her boat for some fishing the next day; something he knew he was going to have to do but wasn't looking forward to. His idea of a good time wasn't sitting out on a boat all day trying to catch a fish. But, in order to catch what he really wanted, he'd probably have to catch a few fish first.

When she said it would cost him a hundred bucks a day he was about to argue her down on the price. Then Mac remembered he was a rich yacht owner and instead agreed. The blow came when he found out they were to go out at dawn. Dawn was something he often saw before going to bed, but never saw first thing in the morning.

She shook his hand before she left, a cool, firm handshake, and then he turned on his stool and watched her as she walked out of the bar. Yes, very nice legs, he noticed, trying to imagine how she'd look in high heels. A rather fantastic rear end, too. He didn't feel so decadent looking at her body now that he knew she wasn't a child.

The bartender came down and asked him if he wanted a refill. A refill of *Perrier*? He had to be kidding. Since he'd concluded his business, it wouldn't hurt to have a real drink before heading back in the direction of his boat.

"A double shot of Black Label," he told the bartender, shoving aside his unfinished Perrier.

"How'd you hit it off with Toby?" the bartender asked him.

"Fine. She agreed to take me out fishing tomorrow."

"Yeah, I figured it was business, or I wouldn't have pointed her out to you. Anything but business and Toby's just not interested, if you get my meaning."

"No, just business," Mac assured him. "Anyway, she's not my type."

"Yeah, well you're not her type, either, if you know what I mean."

"Are you trying to tell me she doesn't like men, or just my type in particular?" He couldn't fault her; he didn't go for the type he was currently portraying either.

"Never seen her with a man yet."

"What does she like, women?" It was possible, he supposed, athletic type like she appeared to be.

The bartender chuckled. "Far as I know she doesn't like men *or* women. She's a real loner, that one."

Well, if she was in the business he figured she was in, being a loner was only common sense.

"Course there was John," the bartender went on in a conversational tone.

"John?"

"Yeah, Captain John Tobias."

Mac became suddenly alert. "I thought Toby was Captain Tobias."

"Natural mistake, I guess, being called Toby and all. No, John took off on a trip once, and when he came back Toby was with him. Been here ever since."

He'd probably been wasting his time on the wrong

person all evening. "So it's John who will be taking
me out tomorrow?"

"John's dead."

The bartender was looking like he enjoyed confus-
ing him.

"So Toby runs the business now?"

"Far as I know. She's a real mystery woman, that
one. Don't get me wrong, she's friendly enough, you
know, but I don't think anyone knows anything about
her. Unless maybe Jay."

"Well, from what you said I don't suppose Jay's
her boyfriend," said Mac, wanting to keep the bartender talking.

This remark really got a laugh out of him. "Not Jay.
He's as gay as most of the *bars* in town. No, Jay owns
the MerlInn, next street over. Toby has a room there
during the summer."

Now that was interesting news, and it meant that
her boat would be unoccupied tonight, and he'd have
the perfect opportunity to search it. He didn't figure
the Cuban kid would be sleeping on it. He wasn't
even sure if fishing boats *had* sleeping quarters.

The bartender left him to serve some customers
and Mac sat and slowly finished his drink. After a
quick glance at his watch, he reached into his pocket
and pulled out the pack of Luckies—which he was
addicted to—and lit one up. Not a bad life, sitting in
a congenial bar, drinking some good Scotch, smoking
a weed. Not a bad life, but he wasn't down here for a
vacation.

Toby wasn't his idea of a drug smuggler, but then
they came in all sizes and shapes. It was her youth,

her look of innocence that put him off. But still he could remember his own college days, and that was usually the age where the spirit of adventure ran high. She probably wasn't even in it for the money, although that would be good. No, it was probably more a matter of thumbing her nose at authority or some such nonsense. Or maybe it was just to support a habit of her own. And maybe she was the wrong suspect altogether, although the investigation had certainly seemed to point in her direction. Well, he should find out something about her tonight and more about her tomorrow. Anyway, that anonymity of hers was the thing; people didn't usually keep a low profile unless they had a damn good reason for doing so. He didn't even know her last name now that she turned out not to be Captain Tobias. He'd have to get a sample of her fingerprints over to the local police and have them checked out. Women her age usually didn't have their prints on file anywhere, but it was a place to start, and the more he knew about her the better.

When the bartender came back down his way, he ordered another drink for the road. The booze was beginning to relax him, but he was thinking clearly enough. He thought maybe he should walk over and use the public telephone on the wall and give Maria a call, but then again he wasn't really in the mood. Why spoil the mellow ambiance of the place if he didn't have to. Lately all they'd done was fight and when she found out he'd left Miami without even telling her, her Latin blood was going to boil.

Mac usually prided himself on knowing when a relationship was nearing its end, and rarely let them stretch out beyond that point. But this one with Maria had been over for months and only his laziness had allowed it to drag on. When women started talking about making it legal, that was when he began looking around for greener pastures. And for some time now Maria had been making those overtures. She might be exactly what he liked in a woman, but so was his second wife, and he wasn't about to repeat that mistake again.

Anyway, and this wasn't just rationalizing, his type of work wasn't at all conducive to marriage and a home in the suburbs. As his first wife had pointed out to him over and over, ad infinitum. When he married her, though, he had still been in law school, and he supposed she had every reason to suspect he'd go on to practice his profession. Two summers of clerking in a Boston law firm had shown him that wasn't what he wanted in life. Not the three-piece suits, not the stacks of paper work, and most certainly not the endless boredom. Well, she had her home in the suburbs now and her two children, as his mother in their infrequent telephone conversations always pointed out to him; so he guessed he hadn't really ruined her life as she had once accused him of doing. His second marriage didn't even bear thinking about. It had been a great affair that quickly came to an end when they legalized it. And then, when the inevitable divorce came, she took him for all he had. Well, he was older now, and wiser; it would be a cold day in hell when a woman trapped him that thoroughly again.

All this thinking about ex-wives was beginning to depress him, and he called the bartender down and

ordered another double Scotch. Mac took a look at his
watch, shook his head in disbelief, then checked it
against the clock on the wall. Unfortunately, it was
correct.

The bar was quickly filling up with people, and the
bartender had no time to chat with him, so he drank
the Scotch in silence, waiting for the drink to lift his
depression. Magically, it gradually did. Great stuff,
booze—it was always there for you when you needed
it. Maybe he did take advantage of that fact more than
he should, but he knew he could do without it altogether when necessary, too. He checked his watch
again, cheated by a minute and thirty-two seconds,
and lit another Lucky. Yeah, this was the life, even if
he was on a job. And if all he had to contend with was
a college-aged girl, the job should be a piece of cake.

He took a trip to the men's room, amused to find
yet another candid of Hemingway in there, then settled his bill with the bartender and left a more than
adequate tip for the man, in appreciation of the information he'd received. Did rich playboys tip larger or
smaller than regular folk? He didn't have a clue.

He left the bar, blinking in the sunlight, then put on
his tinted sunglasses. Another affectation, but at least
they felt better on the eyes. The streets were filling up
with people, mostly young and predominantly gay,
and he noticed a couple of guys turn to give him a
second look. Well, no need to get paranoid—maybe
they were just admiring his duds.

The second time Mac was forced off the sidewalk
by a group of college kids, he turned off Duval and
decided to check out the place where Toby lived and

make sure she was home. If she was, it wouldn't be a bad time to search her boat while it was still light out. It was a lot easier to search in the light than with the aid of a flashlight.

Sure enough, on the next street over he found the MerlInn, and right out in front was parked a bike that looked like hers. He could hear the sound of a piano coming from inside, and he softly opened the gate and walked into the yard. The windows were lit up and he walked by them, peering inside. Yeah, there was Toby sitting around with some guys. It looked nice in there, relaxed, but he had no business being there so he went back out of the yard and headed for the spot where before he'd seen some taxis.

The driver dropped him off at the marina. There were lights in one or two boats, but he didn't see any signs of life and the jetty was deserted. Acting like he had every reason to be there, he boarded Toby's boat and headed down to the cabin to look around. It was quiet except for the gentle slapping of water against the hull. He began a thorough search that didn't turn up anything. A pair of jeans and a slicker hung from hooks on the wall. Inside a sea chest he found some socks, a couple of T-shirts, and a brown sweater that looked like it had belonged to a man. There were a couple of books on the shelf behind the bunk: *How to Reduce Your Thighs in 30 Days*, which he didn't figure she needed, or maybe she had needed it and had now reduced them, and *Decorating Ideas for Under $10*. If she had taken that book to heart he didn't see any evidence of it. The boat was as coldly impersonal as his own had been before he added the necessary writer's tools.

Mac couldn't even find anything to remove that might have her fingerprints on it. There was so little there to begin with he was sure if he took something it would be noticed. Nevertheless, he needed something. In the head he found a yellow toothbrush and a tube of Crest. Very commendable. He couldn't stand the taste of Crest himself, but she was still at an age where she probably got cavities. Mac debated whether to take the toothbrush or the Crest, finally settling on the Crest as it had a bigger surface from which to remove prints. He wrapped it carefully in some toilet paper and slipped it into his shirt pocket. He almost laughed out loud at the idea of being a toothpaste thief.

If there were any drugs on board he didn't find them, but he hadn't expected to anyway. Smugglers usually didn't leave any around for Drug Enforcement Agency agents to find. Somehow they just didn't find it necessary to cooperate with the DEA.

He got off the boat unnoticed, then dropped the toothpaste off at the local police station where they had been notified of his arrival in the area. He found them most cooperative; the Chief assuring him that they didn't want Key West to turn into another Miami. They told him they'd have something on the prints for him the next day, then, when he asked one of the men where the action was, they suggested he head for the Inner Circle, assuring him the bar was straight and not a tourist hangout.

One of the officers even offered to drive him there,

and once he got inside the bar he felt right at home. A three-piece combo was playing old standards, the kind of music he could manage to hum along with, and he saw one or two women who might be willing to do more than just have a drink with him.

Mac took a place at the bar not far from one of the women and decided he'd had enough Scotch and ordered a beer this time. He lit a cigarette, watching the woman through the smoke. She was aware of him, but acting like she wasn't. From her face he judged her to be in her forties, which was fine with him. He liked older women, they didn't expect as much. Black hair, the kind he liked, and a lot of makeup. She was wearing some sort of see-through blouse that didn't leave much to the imagination, and her pants were so skintight he wondered if she could sit down in them. Well, it would be fun to find out.

Yeah, she was just what he needed to while away a lonely night. He even had the perfect line: How would you like to spend the night on my yacht? On the other hand, he didn't see how he could reasonably get rid of her at dawn. To say nothing of the fact that if he had to be up at dawn himself and be at all alert, he damn well ought to get some sleep.

While he was making up his mind whether to even speak to her, she made the first move herself. She moved down the bar, taking the seat next to him, then put a cigarette in her mouth and waited for him to light it.

He obliged, then asked her what she was drinking. He ordered her the banana daiquiri she requested, then, while trying to think of something to say, he came to the realization that he wasn't going to have to say anything at all. The woman was a nonstop talker. In a grating New York accent, she began to tell him what a washout Key West was, how all the men were queer, how her room wasn't air conditioned, how the restaurants all overcharged, how she couldn't even go topless on the beach, how the only man she'd met had turned out to be impotent—and Mac was subjected to the gory details—and how if she had wanted such grief she could just as well have stayed in Brooklyn.

Mac almost laughed out loud at her sad recital. He knew one thing for sure—he wasn't going to be the one to cheer her up. He tried to tune her out, but it was impossible. Finally, on the pretext of visiting the men's room, he beat a hasty retreat out the door and headed in the direction of the marina. He was half afraid she was going to run after him, but a glance over his shoulder told him he had gotten away free.

A mist was rolling in, and a quick glance at the sky told him he'd be lucky to reach his boat before the storm broke. He quickened his pace, his stiff new shoes uncomfortable on his feet. When he reached the jetty it was just starting to rain, and he saw an apparition rise from the deck of the *Free Spirit*. He backed into a shadow and watched as Toby got up and hurried down to her cabin. He had been sure she wouldn't return to her boat that night, and sighed with relief that she hadn't caught him red-handed during his search and seizure.

He went down to his own cabin and got out of his already damp clothes. As he hung up his clothes in the built-in wardrobe he appreciated the electric rod for the first time. The clothes should be dry by morning.

Naked, which was the way Mac slept, he looked out the window of the cabin. Rain spattered against the glass and a small wind moved in from the gulf as it moaned through the rigging of the fishing boats moored to the wharf. It was dry and cozy inside and what would be even cozier would be a nightcap and one last cigarette before turning in.

He poured himself a double and settled down on the bunk. The gentle motion of the boat began to lull him, and he didn't think he was going to have any trouble sleeping that night.

Chapter Three

The missing toothpaste did not go unnoticed. Conditioned to wake at dawn, Toby came out of a deep, dreamless sleep to find it was dark as night in her cabin. Rain was flinging itself sideways against the window like someone throwing buckets of water. Toby crawled out of her bunk, noting the drop in temperature and humidity, and padded barefoot to the head. A quick use of the toilet, then she reached for her toothbrush and toothpaste. Her toothbrush now resided alone.

She remembered very clearly that she'd had at least half a tube left, and with a startling clarity, unusual so early in the morning, she knew that someone had been in her cabin in her absence. Tubes of Crest just do not walk away by themselves.

She took an inventory of her belongings and couldn't find anything else missing, but that didn't assuage her fear. Someone had been in here, and she didn't need three guesses to know who it was.

She told herself not to panic yet. The only reason she could see him stealing her toothpaste would be to lift her prints from it, prints that, to her knowledge, weren't on file anywhere. Of course she had to consider that at the time she vanished prints of hers could have been lifted from the house, but it was more likely that hadn't been done. To her knowledge the police didn't go around taking prints from houses of vanished wives. And in his position, she wasn't even sure her husband would have called in the police.

Yet there could be no other reason for the theft of the toothpaste. The man was clearly some sort of private detective posing as a writer, and he had just as clearly tracked her down. That's if she was lucky. If she was unlucky, he was there to do more than just find her. Toby had actually begun to feel a sense of security in the past couple of years. Now she realized how illusory that sense of security had been.

And yet, it wouldn't do to panic; he couldn't be absolutely sure. She didn't look the same, she didn't dress the same, she didn't even act the same. There might be similarities between the way she was now and the way she used to be, but there must be thousands of other women with the same similarities, and she had always thought Key West would be the last place a Californian would be expected to run off to, taking into consideration the way the average Californian felt about Florida.

If she kept her head, she should be able to fool him. If she wasn't successful in this, she could always try a bribe. Although from the looks of that yacht her husband was already bribing him outrageously. Well, she'd always had a contingency plan for just such an eventuality. If worse came to worse....

"Hey, Toby—it's not a good day for the fishing."
Rico entered the cabin looking like a drowned rat, a
soaked bakery bag in his hand.

"We'll see if our eager fishermen show up," she
told him, sitting down on the edge of her bunk to put
on her shoes. "You didn't take my toothpaste, did
you, Rico?"

He looked at her as though she were crazy. "What
would I want with your toothpaste?" He went to the
galley and put the rolls in the refrigerator. "Maybe
we'll get a day off, eh, Toby?"

She was pretty sure her first charterer would skip
the fishing; she was equally sure that Mac wouldn't.
Especially since it wasn't fish he was after.

She put a pot of coffee on the stove, then got into
her slicker and rain hat and went up on deck. The
other fishing boats hadn't stirred yet, and there were
no signs of activity along the quay. There was a light
on in the cabin of the yacht, however. She was glad
that he would be going out with them. It seemed easier to face the enemy than to worry about what he was
doing behind her back.

She and Rico were in the cabin drinking black coffee and chewing on soggy Cuban rolls when a creak-
ing on the deck told her someone had boarded the
Free Spirit.

"One of the suckers showed up," remarked Rico,
clearly disappointed that he wasn't going to get the
day off.

"Ahoy, anyone on board?" She already hated the
sound of his voice.

"Go tell him to join us for some coffee," she said

to Rico, as anything else would have been out of character. Rico had never seen her act rude with a client and she didn't want anything to appear different.

Moments later Mac and Rico entered the cabin and Toby handed Mac the cup of coffee she'd already poured for him. "Sugar or cream?"

"Black's fine," he told her, his expensive clothes already as wet as Rico's.

"There's supposed to be another man," she said, "but he probably won't show up."

"We still going out?" he asked her.

"If you want. It might be a good idea to wait a little and see if the storm lets up. On the other hand, it could clear up when we get offshore."

He sat down on a bench attached to the wall and held his cup between his two hands. "Whatever you say—you're the captain."

"We'll give the other man ten more minutes and then take off," she said, feeling churlish enough to want to see how the detective would fare in a storm. Maybe she'd get lucky and it would be a really bad storm; so bad that the man might be swept off the deck and disappear into the sea. Then such thoughts, or the fact that she could have such thoughts, began to frighten her, and she looked down to see her own cup shaking in her hands.

Mac didn't notice, but Rico, with his cat's eyes, missed nothing. "What's the matter, Toby, you have a bad night?"

She could almost see Mac's ears standing up at this. "No, Rico—very uneventful. How about you?"

"Oh, you know, Toby—a little of this, a little of that."

She thought it best not to inquire into the details. Rico stayed just barely on the side of the law with the various con games he played with the tourists. He hustled them at pool at the Green Parrot where one of his uncles tended bar; was not adverse to sitting in on poker games in the back room at Carney's; could often be seen on street corners selling tourist paraphernalia at greatly marked-up prices, and lately dropped hints of a tour of gay bars he conducted. She often caught him talking in businesslike tones to her clients, selling them information on where to go to get what they wanted. She worried for his welfare and also worried that he'd bring the police down on her boat, but he'd been irrepressible the times she'd tried to talk to him. Also, he seemed to sense that she had something to hide, which made him view her as an ally of sorts.

Furthermore, she didn't feel she was the boy's keeper. He had a father and mother, numerous older brothers and sisters and other assorted relatives. She was his employer and friend. On occasions when he'd ask for advice she'd give it; on other occasions she stifled her urge to give unasked for advice. In return he respected her privacy.

She saw Mac looking at his watch. She thought he was going to say something about getting started, but instead he asked if she minded if he smoked.

"Go right ahead," Toby told him, going to the galley to get him a saucer to use as an ashtray. When she handed it to him Rico was asking if he could try one of the unfiltered cigarettes.

"How old are you?" Mac asked him.

"Fourteen. How old were you when you started to smoke?"

With a rueful look, Mac handed the boy the pack of cigarettes. Toby watched as Rico bent down for the proffered light, then caught Mac's eye.

"How about you? You want one, too?" he asked her.

Want one? It went past wanting; she had craved one now for eight years, but she shook her head no. Smoking didn't go with the character she had written for herself. And danger lay in acting out of character.

"Mr. McQuade is a writer," she said to Rico, hoping the boy would be able to elicit the kind of information from him she hadn't been able to get. Rico was shameless in his curiosity.

He disappointed her, though. "A writer? Have you seen Hemingway's house?" he asked Mac, who shook his head at the question.

"I could take you there, it's really something. It's a museum now, you know? What about Tennessee Williams? You want to see where he lived?"

Mac looked at Toby and then back at Rico. "As a matter of fact, I would like to see them. When could we go?"

Rico's face broke into a grin at the thought of the tip he'd no doubt get from the gringo writer. "I could take you when we get back today, okay, Toby?"

"It's okay with me," agreed Toby. If Mac was safely off the boat with Rico, she'd have a perfect opportunity to return his visit of the night before. She had strong suspicions, very strong, but before she irrevocably jeopardized the life she had built up for herself, she'd look for absolute proof. Proof she was certain she'd find on his boat.

She stood up and lifted off the slicker that was beginning to make her sweat. Handing it to Mac, she said, "Here, you might want to go up on deck."

"What about you?" he asked.

"My clothes can take it," she said with a glance at his.

"Toby likes to get wet," teased Rico. "You want to start now, captain?"

She nodded. Sitting in the cabin with Mac was unnerving her. She needed the open sea to calm her down.

Toby returned her cup to the galley, then headed for the wheel house. As she went up Rico was already winding in the anchor. She went into the wheel house and started the engines. A moment later she opened the throttle and turned out into the gulf.

It was raining hard as the *Free Spirit* left the shelter of the harbor and turned out to sea. She opened the throttle wide, and the boat lifted to meet the waves with a surge of power. She pulled a hinged seat down from the wall and settled back comfortably, the wheel steady in her hands.

She didn't hear him enter the wheel house, but sensed him standing behind her. She willed her hands to be steady on the wheel as she ignored his presence.

"You think we're going to get in any fishing?" Mac asked.

"You never know; these summer storms generally don't last long," she replied, wondering why they were both maintaining the fiction that he wanted to fish.

As the *Free Spirit* rose to the crest of a wave a sudden squall hit her broadside on and the whole boat shuddered and slid sideways into the valley below. They were thrown violently to one side, and she grabbed for the wheel as it spun and brought her round in time to meet the next wave as it lifted to meet them. In the light from the binnacle, her passenger looked sick.

"You okay?" she asked him, trying to keep any hint of superiority out of her voice. Maybe she couldn't ultimately defeat this man, but at least she had succeeded in making him seasick.

"You got anything stronger than coffee on board?" Mac muttered.

Toby smiled sweetly. "I happen to have some Perrier I got for you." Maybe the fancy water had some recuperative powers she didn't know about.

He groaned. "That wasn't what I had in mind."

"There might be some ginger ale in the galley— best thing for seasickness."

"I'm not seasick. As a matter of fact, I've got a world class hangover."

It was interesting to learn he drank something besides Perrier, which had never seemed to suit him anyway. She had an idea that in another life the man not only dressed more normally, but also drank more normally.

"All I have aboard is beer. If you're having one, would you bring me a can?"

He murmured something and left the wheel house.

She leaned her forehead on the windowpane. Beyond the navigation lights there was nothing, only the darkness and the wind which moaned around the wheel house, filling her with foreboding. Her moods often mirrored the weather, and she longed for a glimpse of the sun.

Mac returned and she could hear the sound of a can of beer being opened. When he handed it to her she took a long swallow. She didn't have a hangover herself, but it still tasted good.

Toby altered course half a point. Gradually, a faint pearly luminosity appeared and she was able to distinguish the dark, silver lances of the rain. Moments later, a belated dawn came and she opened the window and looked out at leaden clouds hurrying across the sky. The wind was fading and already the waves were calmer. Gradually the rain stopped and dawn began to seep into the sky. Daylight came with a slight mist on the sea and a cool wind.

"You're damn good at this, you know it?" he said as her steering evened off.

"You're probably pretty good yourself. That's a nice boat you have."

"I'm not that experienced," he said disparagingly. "Mostly I just live on the boat, I don't take her out that much."

Toby thought if she had a boat like that she'd never stop sailing. Then she remembered that what he said was pure fabrication.

"Where do you live?" she asked him, curious to hear his cover story.

There was a hesitation, then, "Miami." He waited, as though expecting some kind of reaction.

It was possible, of course, that her husband had hired some detective from Miami, but she doubted it. If he did live on a boat—which she also doubted—it was more likely he lived in Newport Beach or some other Southern California marina.

The water was being whipped into whitecaps by a strong east wind that blew steadily out to sea carrying the fog before it. Visibility was becoming better minute by minute, and after a while the sun moved from behind a cloud. She took a quick look at the chart and altered course several points.

Her head felt warm and at first she thought it was the sun. Then she realized she was still wearing her rain hat and took it off, shaking out her hair she had forgotten to comb that morning.

Mac was squinting at her in the sudden sunlight. "How old are you, anyway?"

She gave him a look of surprise at so personal a question. "Thirty-five," she said, quickly adding two years to her age.

"I was sure wrong about you," he said, shaking his head in wonder.

Toby fleetingly wondered if she was now beyond suspicion.

"Yesterday, when I first saw you, I thought you were a kid. Then last night in the bar I figured you for maybe college age. Now..." he let the words trail off.

"And now, in daylight, the signs of age appear?" she finished for him.

"You still don't look thirty-five," Mac said with an unexpected gallantry.

"I feel it."

He laughed, the first genuine sound to come out of him. "Don't worry about it, before this beer I was feeling about sixty."

Probably the stereotypical private eye, she was thinking to herself: hard drinking, hard living, and no doubt with a string of lady friends a mile long. She wondered if, now that he'd gotten her age straightened out, he'd come on to her, but she doubted it. And if he did, it would only be in an attempt to get information out of his quarry.

The wind had dropped almost completely and the sky was clearing fast, but a strong swell was still running. There was something about the close intimacy in the wheel house that was getting to her, a slightly burgeoning desire to confess to the man, to get it all over with here and now. The Raskalnikov syndrome, she thought with amusement. But there would be a certain relief to, at last, put the lies to rest.

Saved by Rico, who stuck his head in the door. "It looks pretty good now, Toby. You want me to drop anchor?"

She nodded in agreement. "And then you can set Mac up for some fishing."

She turned off the engines and followed them out of the wheel house. As she went out on deck a strong east wind dashed spray in her face, but the sky was clearing and visibility fast improving.

And then another spray of water hit her across the front of her T-shirt, and she watched as the thin cotton turned transparent as it clung wetly to her curves. She felt Mac's eyes on her and turned away. A stirring of some old desire went through her. She was usually not aware of her body, but in that brief glance of his all that had changed. She was suddenly cognizant of how her breasts gently bounced as she walked away from him, and how the cold, wet fabric felt abrasive against her nipples, causing them to stand out clearly on her chest. She faced the sun in an attempt to hurry the T-shirt in its drying process.

Toby felt warm. Warmer than the strength of the sun warranted. Well, it had been eight years—a long eight years—and she obviously wasn't the total iron maiden she had thought herself. She caught herself wondering what would happen if Rico weren't along. Wondering how she'd react if Mac were to suddenly come up behind her and slip his hands up under her T-shirt to cup her naked breasts. She remembered a time long ago when that would have been enough to send surges of hot blood through her body. She felt her body begin to tremble and put out a hand to the rail to steady herself. It seemed the years of absti-nence were catching up with her.

Toby tried to think of something else, but it seemed that once she had opened the floodgates of sexual memories she couldn't close them off. She stood now with both hands clasping the rail tightly, willing her mind to empty of such thoughts. Whole scenarios in-vaded her mind, so real that her face became suffused with blood and her breathing quickened. She thought of reaching down and lifting her wet shirt over her head, then walking over to Mac, offering herself to him. Pulling his head down to one swollen nipple and arching her back as he took it between his teeth. She thought of him coming up behind her as she stood there, molding his hard body to hers, his hands moving relentlessly inside her clothes to find her secret places, feeling his answering excitement pressing into her. She let out a soft moan that was drowned by the wind, then beat a hasty retreat to the head to throw some cold water on her face.

How could she even think of sex with a man who was out to destroy her? But she knew it wasn't personal; it could have been any man. It had been too long and she wasn't made of ice after all.

And maybe too, it was the impending sense of danger. She had read that danger acted as a sexual stimulus to some people, and perhaps that was true of her. As a theory, it was psychologically sound. The hunter and the hunted, the prisoner and the guard, the kidnapper and the kidnapped, the hijacker and the hijackee—all sexual situations in the end. And with her personal sexual background it might be inevitable.

She changed into a dry T-shirt and combed her hair, then applied some Chapstick to her lips. She decided she'd had enough beer for the day and took another cup of coffee with her when she returned to the deck.

Mac was in one of the fishing seats, his pole in place, a look of total boredom on his face. Rico was fishing too and she suddenly had no desire to fish herself. Feeling herself drawn to Mac, as though the fantasies had been reality, she sat down about a foot from him and dangled her legs over the side of the boat.

He looked amused as his knowledgeable eyes took in her fresh T-shirt. The stirring began again and she folded her arms across her chest as though for protection.

He had taken off the slicker and his shirt, and his tanned chest, smooth and muscular beneath a layer of glistening sweat, rose and fell with the same rhythm as the boat.

Toby turned her eyes to the sea and noted the storm clouds building up to the south and west. A sudden motion to her right caught her eye and she turned in time to see Rico pulling in a good-sized swordfish, unusual for daylight fishing. You usually had to go out at night to catch the swordfish, but the dawn had been late in coming and maybe the fish was confused.

You're confused, she told herself, to be thinking of fish as humans. She couldn't seem to help it, though. There had been a time when fish was just food, something to be ordered in a restaurant, and she had liked fish in those days. Now she had lost her taste. It was partly because now she did give them human attributes, admiring the clever ones who avoided her bait, proud of the fighters who didn't give up their lives without a fierce struggle. She could pull them in, she could knock them over the head and kill them, she could clean them. What she could no longer do was eat them.

It was a large swordfish and would make a good meal for Rico's family. He was as delighted as a child as he reeled it in over the side of the rail, then held it down by the tail with his foot as Toby knocked it over the head until it was stilled. She removed the hook from the mouth, then handed it to Rico to put in the well.

She thought he was reaching into his shirt pocket

beside him on the deck to get his cigarettes, and didn't react until she saw the flash of light on metal.

"Hold him up, Rico, and I'll get a picture of him," he was saying, a small, expensive-looking camera held in his hands.

Rico was holding the fish by the tail, posing proudly for the picture, although it wasn't the largest fish he had ever caught. Toby felt herself freeze, then reacted instinctively when Mac moved the camera a few degrees and unexpectedly snapped a picture of her. She flew at him, wresting the camera from his hands and flinging it over the side of the boat.

For a moment there was a stunned silence as Rico stared at her in disbelief.

"That looked like an expensive camera, Toby," the boy finally said, judging everything in dollars and cents.

She was clutching the rail, again wishing a giant wave would appear and wash them all over the deck. She knew she should make some kind of explanation or at least an apology, but the words wouldn't seem to form in her mind. All she knew was that she had sensed danger and eliminated it. No matter what the consequences, a picture could not be allowed to be taken of her.

"Toby doesn't like having her picture taken," Rico was saying to Mac.

"No kidding," said Mac under his breath.

"It's just a personal thing with her, you know?"

"I'll reimburse you for the price of the camera," Toby finally thought to say. Much easier than an explanation of her action.

"I'll just take it out in charter fishing," Mac said, acting nicer about it than she would have done under the circumstances.

"What was the price?"

"About two hundred dollars."

"Then today's on me and I'll pay you an additional hundred."

"Never mind the money, I'll go out with you another day."

"I'm booked up for the weekend."

"I'll be around for a while."

Rico was already baiting his hook and casting out and Mac sat back down and joined him. Toby, disturbed by the fact that she'd have to spend another long day in his company, went down to the galley and began to prepare their lunch. She sliced three fresh Cuban rolls in half, then made sandwiches of thick slices of ham and cheese. She took the sandwiches, along with three cans of beer, up on deck but sat away from Mac and Rico while they ate.

The sun was hot and she would have liked to go for a swim off the boat. Nothing, however, would have induced her to appear before Mac in her brief bikini. He had seen more than enough of her as it was.

She went up the companionway and stood with one foot on the rail, looking out into the gulf. A two-masted yacht passed a mile out, sails bellying in the wind, and a small seaplane crossed to the north, sunlight gleaming on her silver-and-blue fuselage. Plans of escape were already forming in her head. What she would like to do was just take off in her boat, head for the Bahamas and never return. But fifty miles away was not far enough and she wouldn't easily get lost in the crowds over there. No, she'd have to head for some city where she could retain some degree of anonymity. Only cities meant jobs, and jobs meant social security cards, and she was tired of living her life just trying to survive. Toby didn't even have legal papers on the boat in order to sell it, and she doubted the money she kept in Jay's safe would last her for long.

"I don't have any money, love," John had said to her. "I always spend it as fast as I make it. But I'm going to have a will made out leaving you the boat. You'll have your own business that way."

She hadn't even wanted to think of that eventuality. "No, John, no will. I'll just continue on here as long as I can." A will would have meant probate; would have meant proving who she was. How could she prove who she was when she was only Toby, a made-up name.

No one had come out of the woodwork and made a claim on the estate when John had died intestate. His friends, the other charter boat captains, had given him a dignified funeral and a rousing wake, and none had said a word when she went on running the boat, now with the help of Rico. She thought they had assumed she was a relative of John's, and she didn't tell them any differently. Anyway, she kept to herself and didn't socialize with the other captains. Most of them were much older than she was, and except for occasional conversations about how many fish they had caught on any given day when they'd meet on the jetty, she rarely came into contact with them.

Toby felt like a fool. The whole day had gone badly.

First the wet T-shirt, gaining his attention and summoning up feelings she preferred to keep buried. Then the incident with the camera. But why would he want a picture of her unless it was for reasons of identification? She wondered if her husband would even recognize her now. She thought she looked quite different, but she might have looked different at thirty-three than she had looked at twenty-five anyway. The basic bone structure was still there and she hadn't had plastic surgery. Not that she wouldn't have if she'd been able to afford it.

She tried to gear her mind to think logically. She didn't think he'd get anywhere with her fingerprints. She had aborted his attempt to get a picture of her, but he could have been taking them of her at a distance without her knowledge. She'd have to be aware of that in the future in case the idea occurred to him. She had read about handwriting analysis, but she hadn't written anything down in years; there had been no occasion to.

But all of these were minor details. All he'd really have to do was get her husband to fly out for an identification, and she was sure he'd recognize her once they were face to face. She knew she'd recognize him no matter what changes he might have gone through.

Something was nagging at her mind, some small detail that she had overlooked. Something about the Perrier water that had bothered her. What had he said this morning? Yes, that he wasn't seasick but instead had a hangover. And had gone on to have a beer. Then why the Perrier the night before? Could it be that, like her, he was afraid to indulge in too much alcohol for fear of talking too much? Did *everyone* get that way when drunk?

Maybe she should make a concerted effort to come on to him like a woman interested in an attractive man. Go out with him, get him to relax, to drink too much, try to get any information out of him she could possibly get. But this was presupposing he would even go out with her. And yet, if she was his quarry, wouldn't it be just as good an opportunity for him?

She was thinking nonsense: Mata Hari in bed with the enemy in order to elicit information. She'd never be able to pull it off. Her best bet, her safest bet, was to just get out of there fast. He must be very suspicious of her already after throwing his camera overboard. But she loved Key West, loved the *Free Spirit*, loved her life despite the loneliness. She didn't want to have to run away again.

And realistically, what would her husband do to her after all these years anyway? Kill her, like he had once threatened? Force her to go back to him? How could he? She was no longer the docile young woman over whom he could exert his power. She was strong now, self-reliant. Surely she would be capable of fighting him. The truth of the matter was she just didn't want to. She didn't ever want to have to see his hateful face again. Or was it out and out fear of the sexual hold he'd been able to exert over her for so long? She was still a sexual being, God knows; that had been proved to her today.

Toby didn't want to think of anything having to do with sex, it was making her nervous. She watched the storm clouds rapidly building up in the west and thought if she was lucky the rain would come again soon and she'd be able to head for shore. Jay wouldn't have fish for supper tonight, but she'd make sure she brought him a good haul over the weekend.

Toby went down to her cabin to use the head and spotted her latest book on the bunk where she'd been reading it the night before. That's what she needed to take her mind off her problems—good, hard physical exercise.

She opened the book to the diagram showing how long the jump rope should be, then searched around until she found a length of rope. Using her knife, she cut it off quickly, then carried it back on deck. A fish was flopping next to Mac and Rico was thumping it on the head, although she knew he didn't like doing that.

"Look what Mac caught, Toby—nice, huh? If he had a camera, I could take a picture of him holding it."

Toby gave the boy a murderous look and his enthusiasm subsided. A traitor in her employ, that's what he was. But then Rico generally liked everybody.

"What's the rope for?" Rico asked, seeing it in her hand.

"I'm going to jump it."

Rico burst into laughter and she knew he was trying to jolly her, get her out of her bad mood. "That's for children, Toby—my little sister, she jumps the rope."

"Well, I'm going to jump the rope, too." She went to the other side of the boat where she wouldn't be seen. She wasn't sure if she even remembered how to jump rope.

The sky was becoming more overcast by the minute. She held the rope in both hands and began to jump. Three successful times, and then the rope got wrapped around her sneakers, almost tripping her. It would take a little practice, that was all. If children could do it she certainly could. She tried it again, this time making it to five, and then a sudden torrential rain came out of nowhere and she was soaked to the skin where she stood.

She hurried over to the other side of the boat and saw that Mac and Rico had been caught just as unprepared. "Want to call it a day?" she asked a bedraggled-looking Mac whose carefully styled hair was now plastered over his forehead.

His eyes were moving over her body in a way that caused her to shiver. She knew without looking down, that once more her shirt had turned virtually transparent. When she caught Rico eyeing her, too, she turned away quickly, yelling for Rico to bring up the anchor.

Once in the wheel house she turned on the engines and opened the throttle. It was early in the day, but she couldn't wait to get back to the harbor. Maybe she'd go into town and buy herself a bra. After all, Rico was of an impressionable age, and just because *she* found it more comfortable.... And then again, maybe she wouldn't. Mr. McQuade should just learn to keep his eyes to himself. His wet clothes had been outlining his body pretty thoroughly, too, showing her more than she wished to see, but she had the good taste not to blatantly stare.

Rico appeared at her shoulder. "Want me to make some coffee, Toby?"

"Good idea," she told him, "and give Mac a blanket to wrap up in if he wants."

But Rico had already gone and it was Mac who answered her from her side. "No thanks, unless you care to join me, in which case I might be persuaded."

His voice was very low, almost a caress. "Are you trying to flirt with me, Mr. McQuade?" her voice cracking on the words.

He gave a low chuckle that sent a shiver through her. "I don't know that I'd call it flirting exactly, Ms Tobias. I think it was more like a proposition."

The word *proposition* hung between them in the close air of the wheel house. She realized she'd forgotten how to flirt, but in the interim she'd perfected her sarcasm.

"Save your propositions for women who appreciate your brand of charm," she told him, making it very clear she thought those women not only to be in a minority, but also completely lacking in taste.

He was standing very close to her, so close she could smell the salt spray on his body. "I somehow had the idea you were one of them," he said in a low voice, his arm brushing against her hair.

She looked at him and once more his eyes were on her chest, and as though on cue her traitorous nipples became erect. She moved her arms on the wheel to shield herself and felt the blood rush into her face. "Then you have the wrong idea," she muttered, wishing Rico would hurry up with the coffee.

He chuckled and moved away from her, leaning back against the doorway. She thought he had left and looked over at the doorway, her eyes coming into direct contact with his wet pants molded to his body. She saw with alarm that he was as excited as she, and quickly averted her eyes.

"Really? I rather think I have the right idea."

She could see him out of the corner of her eye but refused to look over again. The vibrations of the engines were merging with her body, igniting her mounting excitement. She knew if he were to touch her now, just touch her, she would be lost. It was, she was sure, the natural outcome of eight years of celibacy, and not any personal attraction this man held for her, but nonetheless he was the one there when it finally happened. She licked her dry lips and tried to swallow. She felt in the grip of some heat that was consuming her body. And the worst of it was, he hadn't even touched her; she was doing it all to herself.

Get your mind on something else, she cautioned herself. *He's not some romantic figure, he's a detective, here to find you and to ruin you. He's trying to get to you with sex the way you thought of seducing him in order to ply him for information. He's playing games with you, Toby—games!*

She could feel the tenseness in her thighs as they pressed close together, as though protecting her from some danger. Her heart was pounding, her breath felt ragged, and she was sure he knew exactly how he was affecting her. She had thought she was strong, but all it seemed to take was one tall stranger to reduce her to putty.

"What do you want from me?" she asked him, her voice an agonized cry in the wheel house.

"I think you know what I want." The words ambiguous.

Yes, you want my body, she told him silently. *And then you want to send that body back to a man who views it merely as a plaything, something not connected to a soul at all.*

"Leave me alone," she said in a defeated voice. "Just leave me alone."

"You all right, Toby?" asked Rico, coming into the wheel house and handing out cups of coffee and looking from her to Mac.

She took a long swallow of the coffee, scalding her tongue in the process. She felt the sense of the unreality of a moment ago begin to lift. "I'm fine, Rico—just a little disappointed with the weather."

"Toby is happy when the sun is out and gloomy when it rains," Rico explained to Mac in a conspiratorial tone.

"Oh, is that what you call it? Gloomy?"

Toby felt like throwing her coffee in his smug face. "We will have lots of time to see the museum now, Mac, if you still want to go."

"Of course I'd like to—Hemingway is one of my idols."

Naturally, he's the idol of all macho men, she felt like telling him. What private eye wouldn't view him as a hero?

She looked past him out the window where the beach was a white line of surf fringed by palm trees etched against the stormy sky. The trip was almost over and she'd survived... barely.

The naval station came into view and then she was

swinging the wheel, bringing the boat into the harbor. Mac never moved, watching her as she navigated toward the dock, until she finally cut the engine and steered her in.

"Why the *Free Spirit*?" he asked her as she folded the seat back against the wall and prepared to go on deck. "Is it an allusion to you?"

"I didn't name the boat, she was already the *Free Spirit* when I acquired her," she said shortly, brushing past him to get to the deck.

Rico was securing the ropes as she went to the well and counted the catch. Mac had come up behind her.

"Do you want me to clean them for you?" Toby asked.

He looked undecided. "I realy have no use for them; keep them if you want."

"Surely you have a galley in that luxury yacht of yours."

He shrugged. "I might have a galley, but that doesn't mean I can cook."

"You just enjoy the kill, is that it?"

He grinned at her. "I often enjoy the kill." Once more his words were ambiguous.

She got to work cleaning the fish, giving most of them to Rico and retaining one to drop off at Jay's later.

"You ready to go, Mac?" asked Rico.

"Would you mind if I changed my clothes first?"

"No—go right ahead."

"Maybe you'd like a look around my boat."

Rico looked at Toby for permission. "Okay if I go now?"

She nodded and the boy ran happily after Mac.

The sun was coming out again and Toby dragged a folding chair out on the deck and settled herself in the sun. It was easier to dry the clothes she was wearing than to change again. She'd wait until Mac and Rico headed for town, then give his boat a once-over. Her eyes felt very heavy and she knew it was from the tensions of the day. For the first time since morning she was able to relax and be herself.

Toby came awake with a start when it began to rain again. Her clothes, which had probably dried, were now soaked and since the sun was no longer visible she couldn't tell how much time had elapsed. She was sure it wasn't much, though, as her catnaps didn't generally last very long. Probably just enough time for Mac to have changed his clothes and started toward town with Rico. And if she knew Rico, he'd keep him away quite a while.

She went down to the head and washed her face and hands. She didn't personally mind the smell of fish, but didn't want to leave telltale traces of her visit to his boat. The smell of fish gave her a good idea. She'd take the wrapped fish with her. If any of the other fishermen saw her enter his boat, it would look like she was delivering the fish her client had caught that day. She'd just have to remember to take it back with her when she returned. She was aware from books that she should wear gloves when searching, but didn't think leaving her prints would matter. First of all he already had her prints, and secondly if she was careful he'd never know she had searched the place.

She went up on deck, picked up the wrapped fish, then, not looking to right or left, climbed off her boat and boarded his. As she headed down the companion-way toward his stateroom she was certain she looked both businesslike and innocent.

What she hadn't counted on was feeling frightened. The moment she entered and stood still in the door-way. Toby could feel her adrenaline pumping and al-though she identified the feeling as being scared, she was also aware that it was a pleasurable feeling and no doubt what race car drivers, and others in dangerous professions, frequently felt. It was a self-stimulated high that seemed to make her mind sharper than usual.

Her first impression was one of luxury. It was al-most like being in a house with its sliding glass doors covered with curtains, the couch and matching chairs and end tables and lamps, the beautifully fitted galley. She glimpsed a bedroom beyond and walked into it, looking with longing at the built-in double bed and especially the wardrobe that fitted into one side of the cabin.

That would be the place to start, she decided, and slid back one of the doors and looked inside. A ward-robe fit for a prince was hung inside, each item look-ing newer than the last. The pockets in the clothes were empty, but then they had looked too unused to be otherwise. There were three pairs of deck shoes— all exactly alike—on the floor, and behind them a leather shaving kit.

Toby pulled out the kit and unzipped it. Inside was a handgun. She didn't know anything about guns and didn't recognize its make. What she did recognize was that it was real, and her fear increased. She was sure that he had a license for it—that it was all legal and proper—but that he'd even felt the need of carrying a gun while looking for her, frightened her. She was convinced that a man who had a gun in his possession was prepared to use it.

She debated stealing it, getting rid of it somehow, against the knowledge that he'd surely know she had searched his boat if he found it missing. The idea occurred to her to take the gun and leave the fish in its place, an idea that struck her so funny she began to laugh out loud and couldn't seem to stop. She leaned against the closet door, trying to tell herself that this was neither the time nor the place for either hysterics or mirth, and finally she got herself once more under control. Oddly enough, though, she didn't feel as frightened anymore.

For the moment Toby left the gun where it was and went back out into the stateroom. She noted the books, the travel magazines and the typewriter, but wasn't impressed. The possibility of his being a writer was about as great as her being an eighteen-year-old virgin. There just wasn't any such possibility.

She opened the top drawer of the desk and found, conveniently placed inside, his driver's license and passport. The driver's license had a picture of him looking somewhat younger, although that could have been due to the fact his hair was longer in the photo. It was a Florida driver's license and his address was in Miami. Brown eyes, brown hair, 5 feet 11 inches, 160 pounds, born June 8, 1946. One of her how-to books had been on astrology, and she recognized him for a Gemini, unless his birthdate was as phony as the rest of the license. She thought this suited the double life of a detective, though.

The passport corroborated the driver's license and even his purported profession of travel writer. In it were stamped entries from most of the countries in Europe plus one for Tahiti. If he had really been a writer and had sailed his boat to Tahiti, she surely would have been jealous. But if nothing else the gun convinced her that his cover story had been all lies. Writing just wasn't a profession where a gun was required.

She was also jealous of his phony papers. She wished he were a friend, wished she could ask him how he came by a phony driver's license and passport. If she had means to obtain false documentation for herself, most of her worries would be over. She knew such things were available but had never had the slightest idea how to obtain them.

She put the papers back in the drawer and closed it, then glanced at the piece of paper in the typewriter. And that said it all.

SUBJECT KNOWN ONLY AS TOBY she began to read, and then a voice from behind her said, "What a pleasant surprise!" And she froze in place.

Chapter Four

Walking in the rain wasn't Mac's idea of a terrific time, but it wasn't as though he was going to catch pneumonia in the eighty-degree weather, and ruining his designer clothes wouldn't exactly break his heart. And the kid was all right—a real hustler. He admired such ambition in a kid of fourteen. What had he been doing summers at fourteen? Probably playing baseball in the vacant lot and trying to pick up girls. Yeah, even in those days he'd liked girls.

"How long you been working for Toby?" he asked the kid, trying to make it sound like casual conversation. He didn't have to try too hard, in his profession lying became second nature.

"A little over a year," Rico told him. "Ever since the captain died."

"How'd you meet her?"

Rico gave him a sidelong glance. "You sure you want to hear this?"

Mac shrugged indifferently. "Only if you want to tell me."

"Well, you see, I read in the paper that this captain

had died, and I knew who he was. I helped out on other boats sometimes, and I figured Toby would be keeping the boat and would probably need some help, so right after the funeral I went down to see her, and we hit it off, so...."

"Very enterprising," said Mac.

Rico grinned.

"You like fishing?"

"Yeah, it's okay. Hey, you know what I really like? Sometimes Toby takes me out diving. That's a blast, man, you know?"

"Diving for lost treasure?"

"Naw, Toby isn't into that. We go out to where the coral reefs are, you know? Real pretty out there and sometimes I bring back some coral to sell to the tourists. Hey, man, you want to go diving? If you do, I'll square it with Toby."

It couldn't be any more boring than fishing, Mac told himself. "Let me think about it—I'll be here for a while."

"Where you from?"

"Miami."

The boy's eyes lit up. "Oh, Miami—lots of money up there."

Including the profits on seventy percent of the cocaine brought into the United States every year. Yes, there was money in Miami all right, and it was no longer due to the tourist industry, thought Mac.

"You want to get rich, is that it?"

"Hey man, who doesn't want to get rich?"

"Maybe you can get your own charter fishing boat one day."

The boy gave him a derogatory look. "That's not where the money is. I try to tell Toby that, but she doesn't listen."

Or doesn't want to cut you in, Mac thought. He didn't blame her, though—he probably wouldn't trust a kid as a partner, either. And yet he wondered how she managed it by herself.

They were on Duval now and heading south. Turning off Duval, Rico headed toward Whitehead and Mac followed. He wasn't all that interested in seeing where Hemingway had lived; a house was a house. They passed a lighthouse that appeared to be some kind of museum, then Rico was leading him in through a gate, and more cats than Mac had ever seen together in one place, were suddenly winding around his legs. He reached down to pet one, and a voice said sharply, "Please don't touch the cats."

The voice belonged to an elderly woman who looked like she personally guarded the house. Mac declined pointing out to her that the cats had touched him first.

Mac paid the admission for himself and Rico and the woman took them on a tour of the house. She went from room to room, handing out information about the chandeliers, the plumbing, the ornate tile-work and Hemingway's numerous wives, as though it were all of the same importance. Having ex-wives himself, Mac figured it probably was, in the long run.

Mac finally tuned the guide's voice out, his thoughts instead going to Toby. Hemingway might interest him, but the surprising charter boat captain was beginning to fascinate him.

When he had first gotten a good look at her up close in the sun, it had been a shock. She had been the picture of youthful innocence the first time he had seen her. The second time, in the bar, she had seemed young and clean-cut. Then, this morning, standing near her when the sun first made its appearance, she had suddenly taken shape as a contemporary of his. It wasn't the lines around the eyes as much as the look in them; the look of a woman who had seen a lot. And there had been the unmistakable aura of sensuality about her, seldom found in one as young as he had supposed her to be. The awareness of this in her had triggered an equal response from him, which also came as a shock, because she just wasn't his type. Older she might be, but he still didn't go much for blondes, particularly the artificial kind she had turned out to be. The dark roots and bleached hair had come as a disappointment. Her straight brows and thick lashes had been dark brown, complementing the deep blue of her eyes. Why she went and bleached her hair he just couldn't figure, unless, of course, they had her on file somewhere and she was trying to change her appearance. Or maybe she just fancied herself as a blonde, though he couldn't imagine why.

But dark roots aside, he couldn't control the feeling of sexual excitement that surged through him at that first glimpse of her in her wet T-shirt. Such a simple thing, and yet he had been aroused beyond reason. It didn't make sense. Topless dancers and strippers didn't do a thing for him, yet one look at her breasts outlined against the wet fabric had made him feel like an adolescent again.

He didn't even find her feminine, for heaven's sake! She wore no makeup, smelled of the sea rather than perfume, and she dressed the way he had dressed as a kid. Her body looked hard and muscular, not soft like he preferred. She didn't swing her hips when she walked or give him provocative looks from beneath lowered lashes. She didn't even flirt. She was just a bleached blonde, overgrown tomboy, and she was driving him nuts.

The fact remained that he wanted her, and she undeniably wanted him. It had become glaringly evident in the wheel house that she was as aroused as he, and only the presence of Rico on board had stopped him from making love to her there and then. The two of them had generated a heat in that cabin that could have baked a fish, and just recalling it was making him warm. He'd do his job—he always did his job—but he was also going to have her, and if in the having he, in some slight way, jeopardized his job, then he'd for damn sure make up for it. It might be the better part of job strategy anyway.

She thought he was some innocuous writer of travel articles, she didn't have clue one to what he really did for a living. She probably felt safe in Key West knowing that the agents were concentrated in Miami. More than that, by now she reasonably would feel the need to confide in someone, let her deep, dark secret out, find a soul mate with whom to share her burden. That was only normal. People doing secretive work always felt this need deep down. He would be her lover, her friend, her confidant. And when the time came to arrest her he would arrange a deal for her in exchange for the names of her contacts on both ends. That would make using her all right.

And it wasn't as though she didn't want to be used. Mac had seen a lot of needy women in his time, but none that seemed to cry out for it as she did. He'd be doing her a favor—relieving her pent-up emotions plus getting her a deal when it was all over. What more could she ask? And he was good with the ladies, always had been. He'd bring her around. The enigmatic Ms Toby—real name unknown—was about to meet her nemesis.

He was startled to find he was now standing by an outdoor pool and had no recollection of how he got there. It appeared to be the back of the Hemingway house and here there were also swarms of cats.

"These are the descendants of Hemingway's original fifty cats," the guide was saying, and he looked down at Rico, still beside him, and grimaced.

"I've had enough, if it's okay with you," he told the kid.

"Sure, I've seen it lots of times," said Rico.

As they were leaving the front gate, Rico asked him if he wanted to see where Tennessee Williams lived.

"I've had enough tours for the day. How about showing me where I can get a good hamburger."

Rico cheerfully led him down several streets, then joined him in the restaurant where Mac sprung for an early dinner. Afterward, with promises of further tours on later dates, Mac left him and headed over to the police station.

He walked past the duty officer he had previously met and went right into the chief's office.

The chief offered him a cup of coffee, and Mac drank it while he learned that Toby's prints weren't on file anywhere. Which he could have learned without the necessity of drinking the vile beverage that passed for coffee at the police station.

"All that means is she hasn't been booked before, and if she had I probably would have heard of it anyway," he told the chief.

He turned down an offer to drive him back to his boat, and was sorry he had when he got back outside and found it was pouring rain again. Still, he couldn't very well drive up to the marina in a police car.

Not being in Miami, there weren't any taxis around, so he walked in the direction of his boat as quickly as he could, thinking how he was quickly demolishing the most expensive wardrobe he had ever owned. The boat was not his to keep, but the clothes would be written off as expenses. It might even be possible that he'd like the clothes better when they looked a little used, though he wouldn't count on it.

The rubber soles of his shoes masked the noise, and he saw her through the door of the stateroom before she was aware of his presence. *And why the hell was she searching his boat?* he wondered. It just wasn't possible that she could be on to him, and he wondered how long she'd been searching and what she'd found. She was looking at the documents he had conveniently placed in the desk drawer for just such a contingency and hoped she'd take them at face value. But then her eyes moved to the paper in the typewriter, and he remembered what he had written, which wouldn't do at all unless he thought fast.

The best way to catch her off balance was to go on

the offensive. He'd act like she was there for only one thing, and as a matter of fact, that could possibly be the case anyway. Well, if she were there to seduce him, he certainly wasn't going to put up a fight.

"What a pleasant surprise," he said in a way that he hoped would tell her how pleasant it really was, and she seemed to freeze in place, her back still to him.

Take the initiative, he told himself, and a brilliant move came to mind. After all he was soaked to the skin, wasn't he, and she wanted his body as much as he wanted hers.

With one swift move he lifted his shirt up over his head and tossed it on the floor where she could see it. He saw her shoulders lift as though she were bracing herself, and then she turned around and faced him. She managed to look guilty and nervous and apprehensive all at once, and for all he knew she looked a few other things, but by that time he wasn't watching her face anymore. She was as wet as he was, and his eyes were on her T-shirt that clung to her breasts, and he felt his excitement slowly mounting.

Such unveiled blatancy wasn't his usual way with women. He normally took his time and moved with far more subtlety, but catching her in the act of searching his boat didn't require subtlety, it required the same decisiveness it must have required for her to board his boat uninvited. *On the other hand*, he thought with amusement, *she could have been looking for her Crest*.

His hands were at the buckle of his belt, unfastening it then moving on to the top button of his pants.

"Mr. McQuade," she said in that hoarse sexy voice of hers, "I don't know what you're doing, but...."

He was pulling the zipper of his fly down now, but paused as he lifted his eyes to hers. Toby was trembling and he didn't know whether it was from fear or lust.

"I think you know very well what I'm doing. Don't be shy—get out of those wet clothes."

Her eyes were moving around, as though looking for a means of escape, but he was blocking the only exit, and he didn't think she'd try to get past him.

He was easing his pants down over his hips, then kicking them off so that he was standing clad only in tight briefs—his own, not courtesy of Ralph Lauren.

"I think you got the wrong idea," Toby said, folding her arms across her chest and hugging herself. "I'm really not interested. Nothing personal, I'm just not interested in men in general."

"So I heard. But I don't believe it for a minute."

"Believe it, Mr. McQuade." Somehow the way she said his name made it sound as though she thought it was phony. Or maybe it was just the sarcasm in her voice.

"Honey, what I was feeling in that wheel house this afternoon wasn't one-sided. Believe me, I know what a woman wants."

She turned around and reached for something on the desk, and for moment he wondered if she had found his gun, but when she turned back she was holding something wrapped in paper and he felt himself relax.

"I brought you your fish. If you don't want to cook it, there are some restaurants in town that would be willing to do it for you. I just didn't think it should go to waste."

Fast thinking, he'd grant her that. But then she was probably as expert at lying as he was. "Oh, I'm sure you were going to use that as an opening." He could be sarcastic himself when he put his mind to it.

The sarcasm might have been a mistake, though, because as soon as he said it she seemed to be gathering strength. She stood up straight and let her arms fall to her sides, as though daring him to stare at her again. Her eyes seemed to darken as she said, "An opening? Why would I need an opening with you? I'm sure all it would have taken was a wink. You're obviously on the prowl, Mr. McQuade, but I'll thank you not to do your prowling around *my* boat anymore."

She made a move to go past him, but he grabbed her by the arm and held her. It could be he'd used the wrong approach. He'd heard there were some women who didn't go for the caveman approach, and it might be he'd have to butter her up first. Oddly enough, his excitement didn't diminish at the prospect.

"Maybe I owe you an apology, Toby."

"Apology accepted, Mr. McQuade. Now please let go of my arm."

"I said maybe, I didn't say I was apologizing. Listen, why don't we have a drink? There's something I want to talk to you about."

As soon as he said that he felt her body stiffen, and he knew at that moment she was indeed his quarry.

A mask settled over her face. "I don't think we have anything to talk about."

"That's where you're wrong. Look, it's business I'm talking about now, not pleasure."

Her eyes took on the look of a hunted animal, and

he dropped his hand from her arm and instead rested it in a comradely manner on her shoulder. "Look, this isn't a line, I swear. Come over here a minute and I'll prove it to you."

Toby let him lead her over to the typewriter where he pointed to the paper in the machine. "See? I got the idea last night after talking to you. I'd like to do an article on you and your boat."

For no reason that he could discern, she visibly relaxed. "I'm really not interested."

"But it could be great for your business. People will read the article and come down here wanting to go out on your boat. It's terrific advertising and you don't even have to pay for it."

She seemed to be hesitating. "What would you need to know?"

"What do fishermen want to hear? Where the fish are, how big they are, when's the best time for fishing down here. You know, the usual."

While she thought it over he walked to the bar and took out a bottle of rum. "How about having a drink with me and we'll talk about it?"

Mac was sure she'd say no; make some kind of excuse, but surprisingly she went over and sat down on his couch. "Have you got any Coke to go with it?"

He gave her an easy grin. "Well, that depends on what kind of coke you're talking about."

Her expression was stony. "I don't do drugs, Mr. McQuade."

He almost laughed out loud at that. People who really don't do drugs say they don't take drugs or they don't use drugs, they never say they don't *do* them.

That was the "in" talk of people who did do them. Yeah, she knew her way around all right.

"Good, then I won't waste my supply on you. If you're referring to Coca-Cola, I think I have some in the refrigerator."

He went into the galley and returned with a bottle of Coke. He made them each a drink, hers about twice as strong as his. He needed something to get her talking. Although she'd likely be willing to talk about all sorts of things as long as they didn't pertain to drugs. He'd try to get some background information on her, maybe check her out that way. All women liked to talk in general, but she seemed to be an exception.

He watched as Toby took a sip of her drink and registered its strength. She didn't complain, didn't say anything in fact, and he settled down in his desk chair where he had a good view of her without scaring her off. "Drink okay?" he asked.

"Fine. Is this going to be an interview?"

"Something like that."

"Then would you mind putting on some clothes?"

Mac felt a little embarrassed. He'd forgotten how undressed he was. It had seemed like a good idea when he'd started stripping: catch her unawares and throw her to the floor, or something along those lines. The macho male in action. Now he began to feel like the worst kind of exhibitionist.

"Yeah," he agreed, "I'll be back in a minute."

He went to his cabin and quickly checked his closet to see if the gun was still in place. It was, and it didn't look as though she'd searched that part of the boat before his return. He took out his old blue terrycloth robe that hit him around the knees, and put it on. No point in getting completely dressed, not for what he planned on later.

When he returned he saw that her drink was almost empty, and he moved quickly to refill it for her. Good, that was a lot of rum she'd just consumed. Pretty soon she should be amenable to just about anything. She'd no doubt needed the drink—he probably scared the hell out of her by walking in unannounced like that. He poured himself a little more while he was at it. He could hold it, though.

"All right, Mr. McQuade, what is it you want to know?"

"Come on, Toby, it was Mac this afternoon. And I can't get formal with you since I don't know your last name."

He thought this might elicit a last name, but it didn't. Instead she said, "Okay, Mac, you want to get started?"

He wanted to get started all right, but not with talking. "How'd you get started in this business? It seems like kind of an unusual thing for a woman."

A corner of her mouth turned up. Not exactly a smile, but not the straight line it previously was. "Are you one of those men who think women have their place?"

Who was being interviewed here, anyway? He countered with, "How many of the charter boats in Key West have female captains?"

"I'm the only one."

"I rest my case."

She took a sip of her drink, then set it down on the table beside the couch. "I was working for Captain Tobias, helping out on the boat like Rico does for me. He taught me the business."

"Had you ever been around boats before?"

She thought about this for a moment as though carefully planning what to say. "Yes, when I was a child. But that was sailboats. My dad used to take me out."

"Was this in Florida?" He thought she might say yes, which he knew would be a lie. Native Floridians had southern accents; something she didn't possess.

She took another sip of her drink before answering. "No, in Michigan."

"You grew up in Michigan?"

She nodded. "Listen, Mac, could I ask a favor?"

"Sure."

She reached with a hand to brush the wet hair off her forehead. "Could I borrow a towel?"

"Sure, of course," he said, getting up and going to the head, then returning with a fluffy pink towel. Someone had been having fun with him while decorating the boat. Pink would have been the last color he'd choose.

He handed it to her and she wrapped it around her head, turban style. He noticed that her drink once again needed refilling and he took it over to the bar and made it practically all rum this time. When he handed it to her she smiled at him, the kind of smile someone on the way to being smashed would smile.

"You're not keeping up with me," she said.

Mac grinned at her, then drank down the rest of his

drink and gave himself a refill. Still light on the rum, but he was beginning to feel it.

"What brought you down to Florida in the first place?" he asked her, once more seating himself behind the desk.

"Spring break when I was in college. A whole bunch of us used to come down here, but I was the only one who fell in love with the place."

So far the story had a ring of authenticity to him. The place was full of kids from the Midwest who took their school vacations in the sun. "And one year you just decided to stay?"

"That was after I finished school. I didn't know what I wanted to do, but I knew I wanted to live in a warmer climate. Michigan gets very cold in the winter. Anyway, I came down and the only kind of jobs available were waitressing, so I took one in this little café where the charter boat captains hung out, and that's when I met Captain Tobias. We hit it off, and when he said he could use someone on his boat, I offered to work free until I was of use to him. He taught me the business."

"And when he died he left you the business?"

She nodded.

She was either a damn good liar or she was telling the truth. He knew it wasn't all the truth as the bartender had told him the captain just showed up with her one day, but he supposed it could be close to the truth.

"Kind of a coincidence your being named Toby and him being named Captain Tobias," he said.

"He was called John."

Not really an explanation, but he didn't figure she was going to give him her real name. He wouldn't if he were in her place.

"I take it you live on the boat."

"Most of the time."

"Did you live on the boat when Captain Tobias was alive?"

Her eyes narrowed at the question. "I thought the article was on charter boat fishing. I don't think my sleeping habits need enter into it."

He managed to look properly embarrassed at having asked such a personal question. Surprisingly, though, he found he wanted to know the answer. Well, that was a question better left for asking in bed. And the more he talked to her, the more he wanted the interview to end up there.

"Okay, tell me about charter boat fishing."

This was a subject she seemed capable of talking about at length. Mac pretended to be taking notes as she told him how in the winter months the fishing was best in the Atlantic, and when the Atlantic side becomes choppy, the Gulf side is usually fairly smooth. She went on about the Northwest Channel; protected by mud keys and other islands that prevent the seas from building up. She told him about king mackerel in the winter and snapper in the spring and by the time she got to the summer months he had heard more about fish than he ever cared to hear. It was boring and the only thing that kept him interested was her low, sexy voice and the way her T-shirt was drying molded to her curves.

In the middle of her little speech, he found his

drink was empty and went over to the bar to freshen it. When he returned she was holding an empty glass, too, and she didn't even murmur a protest when he took it away to refill it once again. If he was calculating right, this one should be her downfall.

She finally wound down her story and sat staring at him over the rim of her glass. "How about you, Mac? Always lived in Miami?"

"All my life," he lied easily.

"I just ask because you seem to have a New England accent."

He thought he'd lost that accent years ago. Well, give her points for having a good ear. "My parents are from New England—I probably picked it up from them."

"Did you always want to be a writer?"

He nodded. "Always thought it beat working for a living."

"You must do pretty well with those travel articles of yours to afford a boat like this."

A new tack came to him, and he took the plunge. "I've always had a boat, but not in this class. But when you have your own boat, particularly in Miami, other lines of work sometimes happen along. More lucrative lines, if you know what I mean."

He had meant to force some reaction from her, but instead got no reaction at all. "You mean smuggling?"

He admired her guts for bringing it out in the open like that. "Let's just leave it at 'more lucrative lines.'"

"Did you tell Rico?"

Now what was she getting at? "*Rico*? Why should I tell Rico?"

She shrugged. "He likes suggesting to me that there are better ways to make money. I'm surprised he hasn't asked to work for you already. His ambition is to go to Miami, where the big money is. His words, not mine."

"He seems like an ambitious kid."

"Oh, that he is," Toby said, making it sound as though she weren't.

"And what about you? No further ambitions?"

"I'm very happy with my life, very content. And I'd be very unhappy if anything were to change it."

It sounded like a warning to him, but Mac took no heed. "How can you be happy and content in a life that's all work. Hard work at that, with probably no opportunity to get ahead."

"I make enough money for my needs."

"And you have no desire to make more?"

She took a long swallow of her drink. "I think you're talking about illegal means. As I've pointed out to Rico, you can't spend money while you're in jail."

He'd give credit where it was due. She lied every bit as well as he did. "Are you really happy and content with a life that, uh, a life where you don't...." He couldn't figure out how to phrase it.

Toby looked mildly amused. "Are you asking me how I can live without sex?"

"As a matter of fact—"

She laughed. It was the first time he had heard her laugh, and it was deep and throaty and altogether as delightful as her voice. "It's really no hardship, you know."

"I would find it a hardship."

"Well, I'm sure you don't do without."

Mac didn't plan on doing without tonight, either. A familiar stirring in his groin told him the attraction was still there, and talk about sex wasn't helping any.

"All you're doing is suppressing it, you know."

"We have to suppress lots of things in life," she said, giving the words more than one meaning.

"Perhaps, but you're not suppressing it as successfully as you think."

Her easy familiarity of a moment before ceased. "You don't know what you're talking about."

"I know what was happening between us on the boat today, and I also know it's still happening."

"Nothing's happening," Toby said, but he saw that in direct opposition to her words, her nipples were starting to rise. He crossed his legs as he felt his arousal grow. He didn't know why he wanted this woman so damn much, but his body was sure as hell telling him he did. As though reading his thoughts, she took the towel off her head and leaned over, drying her hair in an attempt to mask herself from his view.

It didn't work. Mac now watched as her breasts bobbed from the motion of her arms, and it took all his self-control to remain seated in the chair. When she finally stopped rubbing her head her hair was sticking straight up in spots.

"Do you have a comb I could use?" she asked him.

He pulled his robe around him as he went once again to the head and returned with a comb. He must be making her very nervous; her drink was down to the last drop.

While Toby combed her hair he made her a fresh drink, then freshened his own. He saw that it was almost dark out and a mist was rolling into the harbor. It would be romantic making love on a boat to the gentle rhythm of the water. And yet it wasn't romance that he felt with her, it was more like pure, unadulterated lust.

Her hair was shining when she had finished combing it and only the dark roots spoiled the effect of the golden cloud around her head. She would really be stunning if she'd just take the time to fix herself up. But if she didn't like men, why bother?

"I want to make love to you," he said, the words coming unbidden and spoken out loud before he could put a harness on his thoughts.

Startled eyes flew to his and her soft mouth hung open.

"I want you. And if I'm not mistaken, it's only slightly more than you want me."

Toby got to her feet and he could see she was trembling. "I think I'd better go now."

He headed her off at the door, blocking her exit. He undid the tie on his robe, then shrugged out of it and let it fall to the floor. Still blocking her, he pushed down the waistband of his briefs and bent down to pull them off. When he straightened back up her eyes looked terrified. But behind the terror there was something else, and he knew that something was desire.

"Please let me go," she whispered, but already his

hands were up under her wet shirt and covering her firm, round breasts. Hard nipples pressed against his palms as he squeezed them, and he felt all the fight go out of her as she leaned into him, her eyes turning shadowy.

Mac grasped the thin material of her T-shirt at the neckline and ripped it apart and he got his first glimpse of her dark nipples against the tanned skin. Skin with no bathing suit marks, and he wondered briefly about that. Maybe he was wrong about her. Maybe she sunbathed in the nude and flirted with every tourist she met. Not that it mattered. That he wanted her was all that mattered.

His thumbs and forefingers began to pull at her nipples, making them even longer and harder, and she gave a shudder and arched her back so that her breasts were thrust forward into his hands. They were even more beautiful than he'd thought when he'd first seen them outlined against her wet shirt. High on her chest, they were firm and rounded with just the slightest dip from the pull of gravity. They were the kind of breasts he could get lost in if he let himself.

Her mouth looked soft and vulnerable and he pulled her to him, closing his mouth over hers and forcing his tongue inside to explore its depths. After a moment, she returned his kiss with a hunger that matched his, a hunger he knew had been there all along just waiting to be appeased. She was writhing in his arms, rubbing her breasts against his chest as he sucked her tongue into his mouth and his hands moved down to cup her rear end. He pulled the lower part of her body close to his, then annoyed at the feel of her shorts, quickly undid the button and unzipped them, pushing them down over her thighs.

He glanced down and saw that she was wearing white cotton underpants, the kind that children wear, and he found them ten times as sexy as the frilly bikinis he was used to seeing on women. There was something about the little-girl look on a grown woman that excited him.

One hand slid inside her pants and cupped her buttocks as the other slid back to one breast. He was ready to sink to the floor with her and make love to her there, but instead he lifted her up in his arms, their mouths still fastened together as though fused, and carried her into his cabin. He lowered her body to the bed, then reached down and pulled off her shorts and then her panties. And there he found a surprise, although he was too excited to take in all the ramifications at once. But, from the looks of her body, she was a natural blonde. Unless she did some bleaching down there, which he didn't think was likely. Her hair was soft and silky and as golden as the hair on her head.

Mac got beside her on the bed and their mouths met again as his hands explored the unfamiliar contours of her body. It was a perfect body, all of a piece, the tan extending from her toes to her hairline, and as smooth as satin to the touch. Her mouth was responding to his, and so was her body, but her arms were by her side and she wasn't touching him. He didn't think it was shyness, because she didn't seem to mind how he touched her, in fact she welcomed it, but her hands refused to do any exploring of their own.

He broke his mouth away from hers and looked down at her. Her blue eyes looked unfocused. "Touch me," he said to her. "I don't care how or where, but touch me. Scratch me if you want, hurt me, but let me feel you touch me, Toby."

Her mouth was reaching for his, and once more their tongues were waging battle, only now her hands, tentative at first, were moving along his body. And then, without any warning, she was like a caged animal set free. Her hands were all over him, gentle at times, ravenous at others, and he thought she was the most physical creature he had ever been with. His own was a deeply sexual nature, but he'd never found his match in a woman before. It was as though she wanted to devour him, and he hoped it was really him and not all the rum he had poured into her that was the cause.

She was igniting him quickly, and he moved his mouth from hers and let it travel slowly down to her chest, to the ripe nipples he was longing to taste. His mouth took one in, while his hand went to the other in an impassioned caress. At the first touch of his mouth her leg flung itself across him and his free hand went down to settle amongst the wetness of her silky hair. He tried to consume her with his mouth, his teeth teasing the hard nipple, while their bodies pressed so closely together they almost coalesced. At one point, she wound her arms around his neck and pulled his head down so hard against her breasts he thought he'd crush them, but she only cried out with the pleasure of it.

Toby's head was tossing from side to side in total

abandon as Mac lifted his head to move to the other nipple, her back arched away from the bed to accommodate him. She was murmuring something over and over again, but the words were indistinguishable, and he paid them no heed. She was his now, all his, and he was luxuriating in the knowledge.

When Toby's body assumed an urgency he could no longer control with kisses and caresses, he lifted himself over her and looked down at her face. Her eyes met his and she gave a barely perceptible nod as though to tell him she was ready.

His arms holding the weight of his body, he leaned down to kiss her as he sought entrance to her body. Their lips' fusing coincided with that of their bodies, and he felt her sharp intake of breath as he entered. He began to move slowly, as slowly as the rocking of the boat in the water beneath, and her hands reached up to trace the contours of his face, a simple gesture but one that felt immensely erotic to him. Then, as her body met his with a quickening momentum, he lifted himself up and began to thrust deeply into the warm recesses of her body.

Toby's body rose to meet his as her strong legs wound themselves around his back, urging him on. Mac needed no urging, only the look of wonder that he saw upon her face. He thought he had never seen a face so beautiful in his life, the eyes wide in awe, the lips softly parted. He rode the crest with her and at the final moment, when they crashed down safely on the other side, he was amazed to see a smile on her face, a smile so full of joy that he felt his own lips widening in response.

Why don't women always smile like that, he found himself wondering. *Why isn't it always the happiest moment of all?*

He lowered himself onto her body, his arms holding her to him tightly as though, if he let loose, she might drown. This was the moment when they all spoke of love, of commitment; it was always the same. It seemed to be a part of sex for women, that need to be reassured. But this one said nothing. She lay in his arms with the same sweet contentment he was feeling, and only the flutter of her eyelashes against his shoulder told him that she was still awake.

Mac thought he had never known such an overwhelming passion before, and wondered why he hadn't.

Chapter Five

It wasn't supposed to be like this.

It was supposed to be a seduction scene: getting him drunk, remaining sober herself, taking control of the sex and then, afterward, in the lazy way of lovers post sex, elicit the information from him that she desperately needed.

It hadn't quite worked out that way.

Oh, at first it had gone well. Toby thought she had taken the shock of his entry with aplomb. She hadn't panicked, hadn't blurted out her guilt. Indeed, she had acted as cool as he, and his pretense—of her being there for illicit purposes didn't fool her in the least.

She had had a bad moment when he began to strip. Except for the two scars on the right side below his rib cage, he had the kind of lethal body she was attracted to. Not an ounce of fat, just slim and muscular with the bare minimum of hair. She had felt a response in her own body, and for one brief moment she had fought the impulse to throw off her clothes with abandon and just enjoy the moment. Thankfully that moment had passed.

The ruse of the interview had been good thinking on his part and she'd almost applauded him. It was then she had decided to seduce Mac. Not that he wasn't already willing and had even instigated it himself, but this time it would be on her terms, at the time selected by her. But first she would get him drunk.

She took the proffered drinks, fielding his questions with a background story on herself that he didn't seem to dispute. Of course, they both knew it was lies, but could he be absolutely sure? What did he know about her so far, other than the fact she was about the right age and living alone? That could apply to millions of women. He couldn't be absolutely sure; not yet he couldn't.

Toby had gotten rid of the first drink when he left the stateroom to put on his robe, the second when he got her a towel, and one when he went to get her a comb. A fourth drink she had dumped beneath the cushions of the couch. She hated ruining the upholstery, but by then he was serving her straight rum and she wasn't about to take any chances. And as far as she could determine he had finished all of his. She was sure this gave her the advantage.

She thought she was ready for him, but when he made his move it was obvious who was in control, and it wasn't her. The touch of his hands on her bare breasts nearly paralyzed her, and when he pulled on her nipples it triggered an alarm system throughout her body, leaving her weakened and aroused. So much for eight years' abstinence. She'd probably have been better off taking the occasional man.

She'd thought she was different these days from the young married woman she had been. She thought she was stronger, more in control of herself, and perhaps in ways she was. But not in the basic ways, not in the way her body reacted to the touch of a man, and it was dismaying to learn, dismaying and a little frightening, that sex could still enslave her to some degree. Not by chains or ropes or manacles, just by the right touch properly placed. There was more to be said for conditioning than she would ever have imagined.

Toby was as enraptured as ever when Mac carried her into his cabin and lowered her to the bed. She was his at that point, and there wasn't anything she wouldn't have allowed him to do. He had been a skilled lover, arousing her to the outer limits over and over again, and when he finally took her it was as though that was what she'd been born for. That a virtual stranger could arouse such passion in her was disquieting.

And now his body was resting on top of hers, his hand gently smoothing her hair. It was time for the intimate questions, the aftermath of sex, and yet she found she couldn't summon the urgency any longer. All she really wanted to do was make love again.

Mac rolled over on his back, one arm still around her, and reached to the shelf behind the bed for a pack of cigarettes. He took one, lighting it before offering the pack to her. She took one out of the pack and waited for him to light it for her.

"I thought you didn't smoke." Despite what he thought, he lit it anyway.

"I don't," Toby said, but she couldn't help remembering the good taste of a cigarette right after sex. She inhaled it deeply, but all she felt was a burning in her throat and not even the taste was pleasurable. She almost laughed out loud. For eight years she thought she'd been dying for a cigarette, that all it would take was one single puff and she would be hooked again. Instead she could hardly wait to put it out. She did so, and saw his look of amusement.

"Good for you. It's a bad habit to start, I wouldn't recommend it."

"Then why do you smoke?"

"I'm trying to cut down. I'm down to one every half hour and when I've got that licked I'll go to one an hour."

Which, she supposed, accounted for the way he was always looking at his watch.

Her fingers moved to lazily trace the scars beneath his rib cage. "How did you get these?" she asked, thinking it an innocent enough question. Surely any woman going to bed with him would ask the same thing.

"Got in a fight once," was all he said.

Which could very well be the truth. They looked like old knife wounds, ones that had required stitches. "Do you get in a lot of fights?"

"Not if I can help it."

Toby wasn't very good at this questioning-in-bed business. She couldn't think of any roundabout way to find out what she needed to know, and for that matter he didn't seem inclined to talk. Nor did he seem in the least drunk, although she'd watched him down his drinks.

"You married?" Just get him talking and maybe she'd learn something.

"Do I act married?"

She looked over at him. "You don't think married men fool around?"

"I didn't."

"Then you've been married?"

"Twice. Never again."

Amen to that, she thought. "But you don't do without women, I'm sure."

"There's someone in Miami, but the affair is about over, I think."

"*About* over?"

Mac grinned at her. "You could hasten it along if you wanted."

"I don't want. I'm not interested in an affair."

"I think I recall your telling me you weren't interested in sex, either."

She felt herself blushing. There was no way after her performance of a moment ago that she could make that claim again and be believed.

"You mean you'd be interested in having an affair with me?"

His hand moved over to cup one breast. "This was a little out of the ordinary, you know."

"In what way?" Other than the fact two people in bed usually didn't lie to each other about everything under the sun. Or at least she didn't think they did.

"You didn't feel it?"

Toby was silent.

"Look, I always enjoy sex, but this was.... Suffice it to say you make me feel like a kid again."

She gave him a genuine smile. "I was thinking the same thing."

"Well, anyway, that should answer your question. Damn right I'd like to have an affair with you."

"How long are you going to be in Key West?"

"As long as it takes."

"As long as what takes?"

"You figure it out." He turned to her and kissed her on the nose. "Could I ask you a personal question?"

"Why not?" They were all personal as far as she was concerned.

"Why is it that a natural blonde like you has dark roots?"

She could feel herself tense. "I'm not a natural blonde."

His eyes moved over her body then back up to her face. "You could have fooled me."

Involuntarily, she glanced down at her body hair in dismay. Why hadn't she had the good sense to think of that herself? Well, he could just assume she bleached it; she wasn't going to offer some inane explanation, not that one came to mind.

"Listen, it's your body and it's none of my business anyway. Forget I asked, okay?"

"Tell me something, Mac."

"Ask away."

"What if I said to you, right now, let's sail away somewhere together, maybe down to Mexico and never come back. What would you say?"

"Are you asking?"

"Just suppose I asked, that's all."

"Is that what you want?"

It was impossible to get a straight answer out of him. "I just want to know what you'd say, that's all."

"You'd leave your business just like that?"

His fingers were now on her nipple and it sprang to life at his touch. "It's a tempting thought."

"How tempting?"

"I told you, I'm not interested in marriage again."

"I don't want to marry you."

"Just sail off into the sunset with me, right? Don't tell me you're some kind of romantic."

"Not at all."

Mac chuckled. "I didn't think so."

"You still haven't given me an answer."

"Can I have a half hour to think it over?"

"Why do you need a half hour?"

He gave her a lecherous grin. "Because there's something I'd like to do first."

And then his hands were moving over her and Toby found her body was still aroused, not fully quenched at all as she had supposed. And yet, when had once ever fully quenched her? This time they used their mouths, kissing and nibbling and caressing each other's body in a slow, unhurried way that was quite different from their first frantic coupling. She felt more relaxed with him this time, more at ease, and while the same breathtaking end awaited them, the means to that end seemed more intimate and measured.

She found herself becoming attuned to his body this time around, as interested in giving pleasure as receiving it, and when they lay at last in each other's arms, she felt a sweet contentment she'd never associated with sex. A feeling that defied analysis.

"What are you thinking?" Mac asked softly, the kind of question lovers everywhere ask.

"How good it is."

"It is, isn't it? How do you account for that, Toby?"

"I'm afraid I can't."

"Or won't?"

"I guess I needed sex more than I thought."

"That's all it was for you, needing sex?"

He sounded insulted; the old male ego, she should have known. "What was it for you?" Toby countered.

"Maybe a good enough reason to sail off into the sunset with you."

She wondered if he meant that at all, in any small part of him. She also wondered if he was open to sexual coercion, whether he might also be open to a monetary bribe. She didn't have that much to offer, and yet she could sell the boat. Well, no, without legal papers she couldn't sell the boat. And yet if he was even tempted by her offer, then he wasn't totally committed to her husband.

"I'm starved—what about you?" he asked her, bringing her out of her reverie.

"Yes—I haven't eaten since lunch."

"Well, I've got eggs in the refrigerator."

"And you have fish," she added.

He grinned at her. "Only if you'll cook it."

"I'll cook it, but I won't eat it."

"Won't eat your own cooking?"

"I don't like fish."

Mac gave her an astounded look. "You catch them all day, but you won't eat them?"

She laughed. "I know it's silly."

He was getting off the bed and into his robe. Toby, who had learned to be at ease with her body, went out to the galley naked and looked over his stock of supplies. She put the frying pan on to heat, then made a batter for the fish and began to fry it. Mac was whipping up what looked like an omelet, while simultaneously putting coffee on the stove. She found some bread and put it in the broiler part of the oven to toast.

Mac left for a moment and returned with a T-shirt which he handed to her. "Here, put this on."

"I don't need it."

"I do—you're distracting me."

The T-shirt hit her halfway to the knees. She noted that it was not a designer T-shirt; he probably didn't want grease splattered on one of those.

They were seated at the table and she was buttering the toast when he asked, "What about you? You divorced?"

"No," Toby answered without looking up. As though he didn't already know the answer to that one.

"No urge for a home in the suburbs?"

Why did he have to spoil the moment with questions he clearly knew the answers to? It was bad enough that he'd made love to her under false pretenses, why spoil the simple meal they had prepared together? "I prefer my boat to a home in the suburbs," she answered him curtly.

"I seem to have hit a sore spot," Mac said.

"No sore spot; I'm just tired of being questioned, that's all."

"If I'm not mistaken, you questioned me on my marital status, or doesn't that count?"

She looked across at him. "Yes, you're right, I'm sorry. That was none of my business and I shouldn't have asked."

"Look, no need to apologize. A perfectly normal question to ask a man who's just made love to you."

She felt a smile forming on her lips. "Actually, I guess I should have asked you before we made love, not after."

"Would it have made a difference?"

"No," she answered truthfully. How could she possibly let his marital status matter when she was married herself? That would really be a double standard. Not that he didn't already know her marital status; he was the one who should look to his morals. If nothing else, it seemed unethical to have sex with the wife of his client.

"That's honest, anyway. So you fancy married men?"

"I don't fancy any men at all, married or unmarried."

"Maybe not lately, but that hasn't always been the case." His look was provoking.

"You're right, that hasn't always been the case," Toby snapped at him.

He held up his hands in surrender. "Look, all I'm saying is you're obviously no virgin."

"How astute of you."

"Something happened before you came down here, is that it?"

"What do you want, Mac, my sexual history? There were a couple of guys in college, okay?" This endless nagging of his was making her lose her appetite. Did he really think she was so stupid that she was going to suddenly confess? Throw herself on his mercy? If that's what he thought, he was the one who was stupid.

"Well, someone must have hurt you pretty bad to make you go off men. If you don't want to talk about it, fine, but don't deny it."

She gave him a look of annoyance. "Fine. I don't want to talk about it. Do you always cross-examine the women you have sex with?"

"If I were really cross-examining you. . . ."

"Yes?"

"To answer your question, no I don't usually cross-examine the women I have sex with. But I usually know something about them before we have sex, and afterward they're usually more than willing to talk. I find that perfectly normal behavior myself."

"Well, I haven't had your experience—I didn't know that's how it was done." She pushed away her plate of food half finished. The remark about if he were really cross-examining her had made her feel like her food might come up.

"What are we supposed to be, Toby, two ships passing in the night? One fast fling between strangers without even names exchanged? You really expect me to sail off into the sunset with an unknown quantity?"

She gave him a look of loathing. "The answer to all three of the above is, yes."

"You're strange, you know it?"

"If that's what you think, then why am I here? There're plenty of women in town, McQuade, and they're probably all dying to meet some fashion plate compliments of Ralph Lauren."

That brought a laugh that left him choking on his coffee. "So we've progressed to slurs on my clothes, is that it?"

"I guess that's how the successful writer dresses," Toby said sarcastically. Not that he'd know. He'd, in all probability, never seen a writer in his life.

"Well, I've seen how the successful charter boat captain dresses." He lit a cigarette and for the first time in years Toby found herself not coveting one.

"What's that supposed to mean?"

"Don't you ever wear a dress?"

"No, I don't. As a matter of fact, I don't even own one." And if he found the way she dressed so unappealing, why'd he been coming on to her so strong all day?

"Are you trying to make some kind of statement?"

"No. People who wear designer clothes are trying to make a statement; I simply dress for comfort." Which was part of it, but it was also something of a disguise.

He chuckled good-naturedly, seemingly unaware that he was making her angry. "I wonder what you'd look like in a dress and some heels."

"I'd look uncomfortable."

"And probably very appealing."

"Is that what appeals to you, McQuade? A woman who can barely walk around just to stretch her legs out to suit some man's idea of what a woman should look like?" He probably liked pointed bras and garter belts, too. "Tell me something. Do you dress to please women?"

Mac looked uncomfortable. "No. I have to admit I dress primarily for comfort."

"Which is all right for you, but not for me, is that it?"

He was redeemed somewhat by the sheepish look on his face. "Your point is taken."

He got up and began clearing off the table, piling the dishes in the sink and letting hot water run on them. Something bothered her about that, but she couldn't put her finger on it for a minute. Then it came to her: people who live on boats don't let water run like that. Water on a boat is too scarce to waste that way. In fact every bit used is probably used again and again. Which meant he'd never lived on a boat; was only using this one for his job. And his job, she reminded herself, was catching her.

But as long as he was wasting it.... "Would you mind if I used your shower?" Toby asked him. "I don't have one on my boat and I hate to make a trip into town just for a shower."

"Help yourself," he said magnanimously, obviously unaware that he'd be left with little or no water. In fact, she'd better move fast or he'd use it all up doing the dishes.

When she saw the head she once again envied him the boat, even if it wasn't his. If she had just the shower she'd never have to leave her boat. And, wonder of wonders, it had heated towel bars to keep the towels dry. She took a quick shower before the hot water ran out, soaking her hair in the process. But even that wouldn't matter as she'd spotted a hair dryer beside the sink.

Before leaving the head, she looked into his medicine cabinet on the off chance that her Crest would be in there, but of course it wasn't. It was off somewhere being dusted for prints, she was sure.

Toby was tempted to spend the night with him since she didn't think she'd be seeing him again. At least not socially. He'd have to make his move soon, and she'd have to make a move of her own first. She was sorry in a way. It had been wonderful and for a while there she'd even been having good feelings about him. Which only went to show she invariably picked the wrong types of men. It was just her luck to seduce a guy and then end up liking him. Not that the attraction hadn't been there from the start, but she thought she was over such foolishness as having genuine feelings for men.

Spending the night with him was out of the question. They wouldn't get any sleep and she had to be up at dawn for her fishing party.

She went into the cabin and put on her underpants and shorts. She found her T-shirt, ripped down the front, on the floor of the stateroom. She slipped her arms through it and tied the ends between her breasts. She found she liked it that way. She might tear up a couple more.

He turned from the sink and saw her ready to leave. "You're not staying the night?"

She shook her head.

Mac walked over to where she stood and put his arms around her, his head resting on top of hers. The feel of his body next to hers was making her feel warm again, and she tried to back away, but he held her fast. "I think I better go."

He leaned back and looked down at her. "Was it something I said?"

It was more what was unsaid, she thought. And then decided to brazen it out by saying so. "More like something you didn't say, Mac."

She watched for his reaction, and saw it only in the narrowing of his eyes. He was good, this one, at hiding his feelings.

"What are you getting at, Toby? An offer to sail off into the sunset with you?"

She gave him a smile as though to say that was all she had on her mind. And fleetingly she let herself think about it before dismissing the notion as nonsense. She didn't know what to say, so she merely shrugged.

"If I told you I'd like to, would you believe me?"

"Actions speak louder than words." And that was never more true than between them where all the words were lies.

"There's my work," he began, then seemed to realize what he had said. She felt surprise that the devious Mr. McQuade had finally slipped up.

Toby took instant advantage of it. "You mean your

travel articles? I would think you could write them anywhere."

He dropped his arms and looked at her as though coming to a decision. "Running away never solved anything, Toby. Why don't we have a couple of drinks and talk about it? Maybe we could work something out."

Sure, maybe instead of shipping her back to her husband by plane, he would offer to sail her back. That way they could make love along the way, and she'd have some memories to hold on to when she returned to California. Maybe running away wouldn't solve anything for him, but it had sure done her some good, and would again.

"Forget it, Mac—it was a stupid idea. And I've really got to get back—I take a fishing party out at dawn." There was a coldness, a finality to her words that she couldn't control.

"Before you go," he said, walking over to the desk and taking something out of the drawer.

She waited, wondering what he had up his sleeve this time. A warrant for her arrest? No, she hadn't done anything criminal. Perhaps a subpoena.

Instead he handed her two fifty-dollar bills. "Forget about the camera—it was insured anyway. This is for today, and believe me, it was worth every penny."

The insult behind the words brought her blood to a boil, and she wished she could wipe the smug smile right off his face. How dare he imply her body had been worth a hundred dollars to him? Is that how he saw it? Payment for services rendered? It was assuredly not the fishing he was alluding to.

Toby threw the money at his feet. "Go to hell, McQuade," she said bitterly before stalking out the door. *What a despicable way to end the evening*, she thought, a sudden chill running through her body. She was glad she hadn't fallen for his suggestion to talk things over. A man who would insult her as he had just done would stoop to anything to achieve his ends. She felt unclean for ever having let him touch her. The kind of unclean that would never wash off.

Outside a light rain was falling which did nothing for her mood. She wondered how people could stand to live in places like Oregon or Washington where rain was the norm. She hated the rain and cared little whether the grass turned green or a dried-out brown. The sun seemed to warm her soul as well as her body and she felt her best when it shone down undiluted by even cloud cover. She just prayed that it wouldn't still be raining by morning. She suddenly felt she better make as much money as possible in a very short time. She had a feeling her days as a charter boat captain were numbered.

She probably shouldn't even wait that long. His remark about running away came to mind. He must be aware she'd try something like that, and was no doubt watching for her to make her move. If she were smart she'd take off tonight, take him unawares. Only it would be a bit difficult with his boat moored beside hers; he'd be bound to hear her take off.

Also the office to MerlInn would be locked for the night at this hour, and she wouldn't be able to retrieve her money. And she knew from experience that you couldn't get far without money. There were minor little things like paying for food. Toby hadn't forgotten what it was like traveling with no funds.

Maybe purposely, maybe not, her husband had seen to it that she had no access to money and she had never had any of her own. She had had no money, no credit cards, not even a car of her own, and that, in an area where everyone drove, and nothing was within walking distance. The housekeeper had been given money for household expenses, the chauffeur had driven her when it was necessary that she went somewhere—which wasn't often. Everything she wanted was provided for her. Everything but the freedom to do things for herself.

When she had finally left, sneaking out of the house like a burglar, the only thing of value she carried with her was her wedding ring. She had walked long miles to the nearest freeway and hitched a ride with the first driver who stopped for her. If he had been surprised to pick up such a well-dressed woman, he had the courtesy not to say anything. She had him drop her in downtown Los Angeles, an area she wasn't familiar with, but which suited her purpose.

A pawnbroker had given Toby a few hundred dollars for her ring—about a tenth of what it was worth—but she felt in no position to bargain. She found a used clothing store where she purchased the first pair of jeans she had worn since college, a pair of worn sneakers, and a gray sweat shirt with a hole in one elbow. After that she went to a drug store where she made a few additional purchases.

Checking into a sleazy hotel where luggage wasn't a requirement, she undid the coil of waist-long hair and cut it off at the shoulders. She darkened the roots with the hair dye she had purchased, trying not to think about what she was doing because if she did she was sure she'd cry. She washed the carefully applied makeup off her face and cut off the long, manicured nails. Then, dressed in her new clothes—at least new for her—she surveyed herself in the mirror. For some unaccountable reason, she liked what she saw. Instead of the perfectly dressed, perfectly groomed affluent wife, she saw the beginnings of a rebel. Certainly none of her acquaintances would recognize her, and she no longer had any friends. Luckily she had always protected her fair skin from the sun so that now there wasn't even the telltale sign of where a ring had once been on her finger.

She stuffed her clothes and her Gucci bag and shoes into the sack her clothes had come in, then left the hotel and dumped the bag in a trash container blocks away. Her money and comb she carried in the pockets of her jeans. She was still wearing her pure silk underwear, but couldn't bring herself to part with it just yet.

Wanting to get out of the Los Angeles area as quickly as possible, she headed for the nearest freeway and began to hitch a series of rides that would eventually land her in New Orleans. She used the last of her money there to pay in advance for a room in a boardinghouse for a week.

By then her appearance had changed even more. Her eyebrows, formerly plucked to an arch, had grown in in a straight line, and her arms and face had acquired a tan from standing on highways in between rides. Her hair had even lightened in streaks and was no longer honey blonde, but now looked like she actually bleached it.

Toby found there were no jobs for someone with no experience and no social security card. As the end of her first week in New Orleans drew to a close, she was subsisting on only the meager breakfast the boarding-house provided and found she was growing weak. And yet, when things looked the very worst, she still never considered, even for a moment, going back to her husband. He had threatened to kill her if she ever tried leaving him again. While he might not go that far, she knew she'd never get the chance again if she gave up now. She was tasting her first freedom in three years and it was addictive.

Toby found herself down by the waterfront one night—the last night she could stay at the board-inghouse—going from sleazy bar to greasy café, practically begging the owners for a job. She knew just looking around these places that she wasn't the type, even if she had experience. Despite what she had done to her hair, she still looked more like a college girl than the kind of overblown sexy waitresses those places tended to hire.

At the last place, after being turned down ungraciously by the owner, she was on her way out when a deep voice stopped her.

"You want a job on a boat?"

She turned to see a dignified gentleman in jeans and a yachting cap looking at her. "I have no experience in that, either," she told him truthfully.

"Are you willing to learn?"

She liked what she saw of him. There was nothing in his face but a desire to help, not even the slightest suggestion of personal interest. And she'd come to know that look very well.

"Very willing," she told him.

He took up his cup of coffee and led her over to one of the booths. "How about if I buy you some dinner while you think about my offer," he said to her, and she gratefully took a seat across from him and ordered the cheapest thing on the menu. It was eggs, and at this point she didn't trust her empty stomach to anything richer, which is how she ended up as Toby of Key West, Florida.

And while she was always extremely careful, always on the lookout for strangers and wary of forming friendships, still, somewhere in the back of her mind, she had felt that she had successfully eluded her husband, at least after the first couple of years, which made the presence of Mac so much more troubling than if she had still been expecting it.

She knew her husband was nothing if not tenacious and would not hesitate to use his considerable monetary resources to find and bring back one of his prized possessions. That was exactly how he had viewed her; as a possession. And he did not take lightly losing what was his.

She wished John were still alive. While he had never questioned her and she had never confided her past to him, she knew that if he were here now she'd do so and that he would do everything in his power to help her out of the situation. Having no well-formulated plans of her own, she tried to think what he would have done for her. No doubt he first would have suggested she see a lawyer. And of course she had always had recourse to the courts. Especially in California where no-fault divorce was in effect, she could have gone to court and divorced her husband with no difficulty. Except that Toby knew her husband. Knew his pathological jealousy and his vicious temper. Knew that never for a moment would he allow her to be free, free to become the possession of another man. He would have retaliated in some way, and the knowledge of that had kept her with him long past the time she had started to want to escape. He felt, with some justification, that he had molded her into his vision of the perfect woman, and she felt he would kill before allowing another to reap the rewards of his tutelage.

If she went to a lawyer now, her husband would be notified through legal channels, and that wouldn't solve anything. A divorce would mean nothing if he knew where to find her. And a divorce wasn't important anyway since she didn't intend to remarry.

What John might have done, and what she would like to do now, would be to sail her to the Bahamas where it would be a lot more difficult for him to find her, and where the United States had no jurisdiction. And yet her chances of being able to support herself in the Bahamas were nil. Her best bet would be to lose herself in the anonymity of some large city, someplace where it might be possible to buy papers that would establish a new identity for herself.

New York came to mind, being the largest most impersonal city she could think of, but the very thought of having to live in a place like New York filled her with dismay. She would be forever relegated to living an underground existence, taking only jobs where an educational background was never checked and where work experience didn't count. There were many drawbacks to New York, though. For one it would require an entire wardrobe, from shoes to winter clothing, and this would eat up a good part of her savings. And then there was the weather, something she didn't want to even think about. She also didn't like the New Yorkers who came down to Key West to vacation. They seemed a breed apart from other Americans, louder, considerably more rude, the men not adverse to making advances on a female charter boat captain.

Toby would prefer Miami. Only Miami seemed too close for comfort. And she hadn't heard very good things about Miami, either, which as far as crime went was turning into the New York of the South.

She thought of the islands in the Caribbean, South America, Europe. But she'd need a passport for most of them and at least ID for the others. She wasn't sure about the Bahamas. And Puerto Rico, of course, she could get into with no papers. And there was always Cuba, which would be easy enough to sail to, but she didn't like the idea of living there and was doubtful that she'd be accepted with open arms. She would just as likely be thrown into some jail and left to rot.

If only she could sell the boat. The proceeds from the sale would allow her to go anywhere and have enough to live on for some months. But wishful thinking wasn't getting her anywhere. Much as she hated the idea, she'd begin to set in motion her flight to New York. Someday, she would hope, she'd be able to return. In the meantime, she'd leave the boat in Rico's care and only hope he wouldn't use it for some foolishness.

Toby got into her bunk. She knew she wouldn't sleep with so much on her mind, but she hoped to get some rest. She tried not to let her thoughts dwell on the events of the evening, but memories of the sex with Mac kept coming unbidden into her mind. The sex itself had been a revelation. Conditioned by her husband to be the passive partner, this had been the first time she'd given vent to her own desires, and her response had both shocked and delighted her. Allowed to behave and respond as she liked, she had been aware of going a little wild with the new found freedom, but if there had been anything wrong in her wanton abandonment, she hadn't seen it reflected in Mac's face. Placing no restrictions on her at all, he had seemed to enjoy it as much as she.

She felt her body grow warm at the mere memory of what they had done together, and tried to concentrate instead on the steady pattern of rain above on the deck. It didn't sound as though it was going to let up. Perhaps she'd have a free day tomorrow to put her affairs in order and plan her departure.

Chapter Six

Mac awoke abruptly, then reached for his watch on the shelf. It was 10:00 A.M., and still dark out with the rain coming steadily down. He was at zero hour as far as cigarettes went, so he wasted no time in lighting his first. The sheets were pulled out as though he had tossed in his sleep, but then with a dawning wakefulness he remembered how they had gotten that way.

With a smile on his face, he made a quick trip to the head, then went to the galley to put on some water to boil. He was feeling good. Relaxed. Recharged, even. And all due to the redoubtable Toby, his adversary. He looked out the window and saw that her boat was still in port, which meant her clients must have begged off. He had thought confirmed fishermen would ply their luck in any weather, but she probably got her share of amateur anglers who wanted all conditions perfect.

He'd have to call Miami today, find out if they had any further information on when the shipment was due. They had all their sources working overtime on this one, and he hoped they had learned something.

He should also call Maria. It would be just like her to call the police and report him missing, which, when it got back to his office, would make him the butt of much amusement. He'd give her some story, perhaps a not-too-convincing one. He thought she was close to breaking off the affair, and that might be all it would take to pressure her into doing it now. Only laziness and an aversion to volatile scenes had prevented him from precipitating the break-up sooner; although this time there might not be a volatile scene. He thought she was as ready to break it off as he was. There seemed to come a time in every relationship when the woman started making noises that the relationship should move to the next step in a steady progression of steps. He felt it coming with Maria when she began to keep as many of her clothes at his apartment as at her own, and when there began to be talk of two living as cheaply as one.

Mac felt there was truth in that old adage, that two could live as cheaply as one. Unfortunately, two couldn't live as compatibly as one, and he had the experience to prove it. Furthermore, his work just wasn't conducive to settling down. Women didn't take well to living with men in dangerous occupations, illustrated by the high divorce rate amongst law enforcement people. And there was his traveling—usually without advance notice—and the often undesirable characters he had to associate with.

Anyway, he didn't require the usual things from a woman that his associates thought a necessity, the kind of benefits one derived from a spouse. He had a cleaning service that took care of his condo, and he preferred paying for this service rather than having to feel grateful. He preferred eating his meals out. He had no desire to propagate the species and, in fact, felt somewhat uncomfortable when forced to spend any time with his nephews and nieces. He particularly didn't like the absence of privacy; the having to account for where he had been and what he had done, and where was he going now when he'd just returned home. He had never asked those questions of his wives, although they had never gotten the message and reciprocated.

And yet, Mac liked a warm body next to his at night. Liked not having to hit the local bars and go through the long, tiresome process of starting something up with yet another woman, getting into a new relationship that was doomed from the start. Yeah, the steady sex was nice; it just wasn't everything.

He made a cup of instant coffee and took it over to the table. The rain against the window made everything take on a blurred shape, but he saw something yellow moving across the deck of the *Free Spirit.* It looked like Toby in her slicker and hat was leaving her boat. Toby. What a ridiculous name for that woman. Toby should be the name of a little boy, not the sensuous woman he'd spent part of the night with. Toby was going to take a lot of thinking about, and he wasn't sure he was up to it. He didn't have a World Cup hangover, but it sure was a contender.

First of all, why the hell had she been searching his boat? He'd expected her to be somewhat suspicious of him. If he were a smuggler he'd be suspicious of strangers, too, but what did she hope to accomplish by searching the place? If he was what she surmised him to be, she must know he wouldn't leave around incriminating information like, for instance, his DEA ID. If she was looking for evidence that he was a writer, well, that stuff had been around for her to see. Who knows, maybe she just missed her tube of Crest? But why would she think he'd take a tube of toothpaste? It didn't make sense.

Next, there was the matter of darkening her roots. Mac had heard of bleached blondes. They abounded in Miami, but he'd never heard of a natural blonde who dyed her roots dark. That didn't make any sense to him at all. Why would she want to change her appearance unless she had a record somewhere, and he had an idea she didn't. If she did she'd have had to been pretty young at the time, because she'd been in Key West for eight years. Maybe it was a deliberate attempt to cheapen her appearance, make her unattractive to the men she tried so hard to avoid. Who could figure out women, anyway? Except he still found her attractive. Damn attractive, as a matter of fact.

So the hair was a mystery, but one he'd like to solve. Then there was the background story she gave him. Michigan. Wanting to live in a warmer climate. That had all sounded true enough. She probably had nothing to hide before she got into the smuggling. And maybe the late Captain Tobias had gotten her into that. Maybe he had taught her an easier way of making money than just taking tourists out for fish, which, incidentally, made an excellent cover for her real business. He wondered briefly what she did with the profits she made. She sure as hell didn't spend them on clothes. Well, for all he knew she could be buying up real estate in the Bahamas.

The sex part. That was the hardest to understand. Mac had expected that if he got her drunk he'd be able to seduce her, but despite all the rum he'd practically poured down her throat, she hadn't seem affected at all. He had been half smashed himself, despite the fact he'd made his own drinks very watered down. But he still couldn't get over her performance in bed. Because that was what it had to be—a performance.

All he'd had to do was touch her, and she lit up like a torch. There'd been a while there when he got her in the bunk when she'd been rather passive, surprisingly so, since he could tell she was so aroused by that time sparks were practically coming off her. But once he'd told her to touch him she'd gone wild. Just remembering it was turning him on.

He'd been surprised as well by his own performance. Maybe it was the fact that she was a mystery lady, or that she was the pursued and he the pursuer, he didn't know. What he did know was that she'd ignited him like no woman had ever done. It had been like she was his perfect complement. In bed, of course—not anywhere else. But he'd settle for that.

Mac didn't know why he hadn't found her feminine in clothes. He'd found her naked body perfect. He tried to visualize how she'd look in a tight dress and heels, but the picture wouldn't seem to form. The only way he could picture her now was stark naked, and the picture was unnerving.

He'd really been feeling something for her last night. Real feelings, not just the kind you faked when you picked up a lady somewhere. And it wasn't just the sex, either. Cooking together had been nice, as had the little talking they'd done. He'd even given serious thought to the sailing off into the sunset part. The thing was, he didn't think she was serious about it for a minute. She had seemed to be testing him, and he didn't know whether he'd failed the test, or passed it.

There had been a moment there, shortly before she left, when he'd been about to level with her, try to help her out of the mess she was in. She had to have known what he was alluding to, but she'd sidestepped him neatly. The money she had taken wrong, but she'd get over that. She couldn't really believe he was trying to pay her for the sex, could she? No. When you paid a woman you didn't stick around and make breakfast for her.

The fact of the matter was, he shouldn't have allowed himself to become personally involved with her. It had seemed like a good idea at the time, but it was backfiring in his face. Because he didn't want to nail her; set her up for a prison sentence. But she sure as hell didn't look like she was about to cooperate with him, and without her cooperation there was no way he could help her.

She had to be one of the toughest, most independent women he had ever met. So why did he feel like she needed his protection? Why was *he* feeling so damned protective of her? It had been a tempting thought to just sail off with her. For as long as it lasted, he would have had her all to himself, and that thought was more than tempting, it was inflammatory. Just what he needed—the Feds after both of them. His office wouldn't take kindly to his absconding with the boat.

Well, he'd give it another try if he had a chance. If not, he'd do what he could to help her once he'd nailed her. Until then, he better get into town and make a couple of phone calls.

Mac got into his fancy clothes and, feeling a bit of a fool, left the boat carrying an umbrella. He was getting a little tired of always being soaked, though.

He walked down to Duval Street and found a café that served breakfast. While he waited for his eggs, he used the phone on the wall in the back to call his office. "This is Mac," he said when he'd connected. "Got anything for me?"

"Having a good time, Mac?" asked Carol, a female operative who was tired of having to man the phones and longed to see some action. The trouble was, she looked so damned straight they didn't know how to use her.

"Great. Rained the whole time I've been here."

"It's raining here, too."

He couldn't care less what the weather was like in Miami. "Got any more information for me, Carol?"

"Nothing more on Tobias—he's still a blank."

"He's dead."

"Yeah? I guess that would explain it. So who're you surveilling?"

"Calls herself Toby, no last name. Was taken in by Captain Tobias and has inherited the business."

"That's all you've found out about her?"

He didn't think Carol would be interested in hearing how Toby was a natural blonde. "That's about it. I ran her prints through the local PD, and nothing. I have a feeling she doesn't have a record."

"So maybe she's clean."

"No. There's definitely something suspicious about her. I think she's the one, all right."

"One of your informants—Buggy?—keeps calling."

"Not Buggy, it's Boogie. Did he say what he wanted?"

"Said it was urgent, that he had the information you had requested."

"So give it to me."

"He refuses to speak to anyone but you."

"Did he leave a number where he can be reached?"

"Nope. Said he had to see you in person."

This could be what he needed. If Boogie was calling in with what he thought he was calling in with, he'd have the exact time of the exchange for him. "Look, when he calls again tell him I'll be in Miami tomorrow."

"You're coming back?"

"I'll come in on the morning flight and go back on the afternoon. If he can meet me at the airport that would be even better."

"If he calls again I'll give him the message."

Mac hung up and went back to the table where his cold eggs were congealing. He was on an expense account, he reasoned, as he ordered a second breakfast. He lit a cigarette and drank the still warm coffee as he

waited. He wouldn't bother to call Maria. He'd wait
and call her from the airport, maybe take her out to
lunch after he'd seen Boogie. Boogie just might save
him a lot of waiting around and watching the *Free
Spirit*. Not that he minded watching the owner of the
Free Spirit, who, it seemed, was something of a free
spirit herself.

When he finished his breakfast he ordered two
large containers of black coffee to go, then took a cab
over to the police station. The chief was in.

"A bribe," he said to him, placing one of the containers of coffee on the desk.

The chief took off the lid and looked inside. "Coffee?"

"I thought it was a damn good bribe considering
what passes for coffee around here."

The chief was nodding. "You're right. What can I
do for you, Mac?"

"I'm flying up to Miami tomorrow for the day.
Thought maybe you could keep an eye on the *Free
Spirit*. Sort of unobtrusively, you know."

"Nothing's going to happen in daylight."

"You're probably right. Anyway, I think I'm going
to be coming back with that information anyway."

"I'll do what I can."

"Appreciate it."

"No sweat. I don't want Key West turning into
another Miami. Speaking of which, we conducted a
pretty good drug bust last night. If I'd known how to
reach you...."

"Cocaine?"

"Nothing but."

"How much?"

Several kilos. More than I'd like to think is coming in here."

Mac shrugged. "It could've come down from Miami."

"That's what I'm hoping. But in case it's not, you want a go at the guys?"

"You mean they didn't make bail?"

"Not as yet. I've got 'em locked up right down the hall. Better accommodations than you get in most of the guest houses around here, too."

"Did you get anything out of them?"

"Name, rank and serial number, you know the score."

"No connections, huh?"

The chief shook his head.

"Yeah, I'd like to see them. But not officially. Just tell them they have a visitor."

He'd expected Cubans, maybe Colombians, but the two young men shown into the visitors' room were Anglo and looked like they'd be more at home in his Ralph Lauren clothes than he was. In their twenties, they acted cool and wary.

"I'm a friend of Toby's," he said, hoping to get some kind of reaction from them.

"Who's Toby?" one of them asked, and if they knew her he sure couldn't tell by the way they were acting.

After ten minutes of questioning, mostly one-sided, they were still swearing they didn't know a Toby, and Mac tended to believe them. They were also acting like it was only a matter of time before they'd be out on bail, and a lawyer'd be handling the problem for them. Mac was sure they were right.

He thanked the chief and walked outside to find the rain had stopped and the sun was giving off about ninety degrees of heat. Instead of lowering the humidity, the rainstorm seemed to have increased it. If he'd been all alone and not on a populated island, he would have considered using his umbrella as a sun screen. All he needed, though, was a bunch of gays following "the guy with the parasol."

A couple of guys who were prime candidates for heat exhaustion, if not heart attacks, jogged by him, and it occurred to Mac that the people who lived down here, at least the natives, looked healthier than their counterparts in Miami. But then the people populating Miami were either retired folk, tourists down to look for a retirement place, or those in the kind of unsavory professions where having a tan or being fit didn't matter.

As he approached Garrison Bight he saw the *Free Spirit* heading out to sea. He didn't see Rico aboard, or any signs of fishermen, just Toby's golden head was visible through the window of the wheel house. He quickened his steps, wondering where she was headed.

Was she on her way to make the pickup? Maybe heading out to warn someone? Making a run for it? And maybe he was getting a little paranoid. Surely she must often take the boat out for all kinds of innocent reasons. Maybe she just felt like a ride.

And just maybe he ought to follow her.

She'd be bound to notice him, though, and might

that not be showing his hand? He *was* getting paranoid. Surely after having spent half the previous night making love to her it would only be normal for him to follow her out. Maybe they could have a swim together. Maybe they could do a few other things together . . . .

Mac boarded his boat and moved across the deck, pausing in the shadows of the companionway. A distance out now he could see the *Free Spirit* lift on a swell and then subside. She was quite a ways out, but her engines were no match for his; he'd catch up with her in a matter of minutes.

He went down to his cabin and changed out of his sweaty clothes into his bathing trunks. He mixed himself a rum and Coke and carried it with him back on deck. He cast off, then started up the engines. Ten minutes later he spotted the *Free Spirit*, and minutes later he was pulling up to her starboard side. The engine stopped and everything seemed curiously still in the great heat.

More curious, he could see no sign of her. He leaned against the rail, expecting to see her emerge from her cabin at any moment. When she didn't appear, he began to wonder if he was too late. Maybe some cabin cruiser had picked her up and she was now miles away. His eyes searched the water for her bobbing head, but he could see nothing.

Without even consulting his watch, he lit a cigarette and wondered what he should do. She'd been foolish to come out here alone; even on a beach people weren't supposed to go swimming alone. He kept telling himself he was overreacting, but at the same time he wondered if he should call the coast guard and ask for their help. A sweat broke out on his face that had nothing to do with the heat, and he was forced to admit that he cared very much what happened to her, and it had nothing to do with his job.

Without thinking about it any further Mac dove off the side of his boat and headed in the direction of hers.

Chapter Seven

Toby was awakened by Rico's footsteps above her on the deck. She could see it was dark, could hear the rain, and felt like nothing more than turning over and going back to sleep. Instead she got up and pulled a pair of shorts on to go with the T-shirt she had slept in. And just in time, because Rico's head peered into the cabin only seconds later.

"I think we don't go out today," he told her.

"I think you're right. Have either of the charterers shown up?"

"Yeah, one of them came down to tell you they're going to give it a miss in the rain. Said they'll be around another week and will contact you again."

Any extra money she could have picked up before leaving would have helped, but at least this would give her a chance to clear up her affairs before she left.

"Rico, if anything should happen to me—"

"What's going to happen to you, Toby?" The boy looked worried. Far out of proportion, she thought, to her words.

"Probably nothing, but just in case —"

"I don't want to talk about it." There was a stubborn set of his small face, and she realized for the first time that he really cared for her.

"Will you just hear me out, Rico?" She waited for him to interrupt her again, and when he didn't, "I just want you to know there's a letter in my envelope in the safe at MerlInn leaving you the boat and the business, that's all. Do you think you could handle it?"

"Sure, I get my cousin, Mario, to help me. But nothing's going to happen to you, Toby."

"Probably not. I just wanted you to know, that's all."

"Okay, I'll remember. Now can I go? I set up a tour last night with some people just in case it rained today." Rico was always well prepared. No Boy Scout, but prepared nonetheless.

"Yeah, run along — I'll see you tomorrow."

"You're sure you're okay, Toby?"

"Don't I look okay?"

He looked her over carefully. "Yeah, you look fine."

She went to the galley and fixed herself a cup of coffee. She could see a light in the cabin of Mac's boat and wondered what he was doing up so early. Maybe a guilty conscience? She hoped so. What he had said to her had been unforgivable. And yet, to be fair, she had probably deliberately misconstrued his words. He hadn't been paying her for the sex. In a way he had been complimenting her, only she had chosen to take it wrong to suit her own purposes. Which, at the time, had been to get out of there as quickly as possible. He had wanted to talk, and she hadn't been ready for him to bare his soul to her. Lingering around Mac could do her no good at all.

The only thing that would do her any good would be to get out of Key West and out of his reach. She had things she had to take care of today, but tomorrow she'd get a flight to Miami and a connecting flight to New York. Out of his reach, and also out of the life she had loved.

Well, nothing lasts forever, Toby told herself as she combed out her hair and applied some Vaseline to her dry lips. She'd have to wait until she got to MerlInn to brush her teeth; she still hadn't replaced the Crest, and now she'd never have to.

What she knew she was going to have to do was buy some clothes to wear to New York. She didn't know how they dressed up there, but she had a feeling it wasn't in cut-off shorts and T-shirts, at least not to check into a hotel. She might be able to get away with a large tote bag in lieu of luggage, but she'd have to at least look presentable.

Did presentable mean a dress? She hadn't worn a dress in years and had hoped she'd never have to again. But she ought to have at least one decent outfit for purposes of job hunting and the like. The rest of the time she was sure her jeans would be fine. She'd have to try to change her appearance again, but she'd wait until she got to New York. She couldn't do it here and perhaps run into someone she knew. She'd go dark with her hair this time. It would match her eyebrows and lashes and look natural enough. And she wouldn't worry about her body hair matching because she wasn't about to get involved with a man again.

That had been pretty perceptive of him, when she thought about it. But then it would be pretty hard not to notice the other person's body when you were in bed together naked.

A sudden thought froze Toby. She hadn't used any means of birth control with him. She'd been on the pill when she was living with her husband, but had run out of the prescription her first week on the road. And she hadn't had any need for any since. She did some calculating in her head and came to the conclusion that with her period due to start the following Tuesday she was probably safe. If not, well she'd just have to contend with that eventuality when it happened. If it happened. And New York probably had an abundance of women's clinics.

Still, it had been foolish, and she wasn't usually foolish. Last night had been an anomaly, Mac, the circumstances, and the sex certainly out of the ordinary. And yet she had never known the ordinary. Certainly her husband's brand of sex couldn't be termed that, and she thought the kind of fireworks she and Mac had generated between them probably didn't occur too often. She didn't even know whether it would be the same with him a second time, but she wasn't going to find out, that was for sure. Too many good feelings about him had been intertwined with the sex, and she couldn't afford to have good feelings about the man who had hunted her down.

She knew, however, that part of the exhilaration she was feeling was due to Mac. She had dreamed last night, and for a change it hadn't been about California. Mac had figured in her dreams this time rather than her husband, and they had been so pleasurable she hadn't wanted to wake up. And, as is the way with dreams, they were still feeling very real to her. So real that if he were to walk in now she'd probably succumb to the temptation of lying once more in his arms. But, as is also true of dreams, she knew their fragile reality would dissipate in a couple of hours.

Toby wondered what it would have been like to have been married to Mac instead of her husband. And yet, in his own way, Mac projected the same macho image that she'd been so taken in by. And no wonder, what with the way she'd been brought up, she mused. When books and films are filled with heroes who are strong and exude machismo, is it no wonder young women look to that as their ideal in a man? While the nice men, the decent ones, are overlooked. Her husband had carried it to an extreme to be sure, and yet if Mac had indeed been married twice already, there must be something about him that led women to leave him. But early conditioning is hard to shake off, and it was still that kind of man who seemed to appeal to her if last night was any indication.

All of which was a waste of time to think about anyway, and celibacy was still the ticket as far as she was concerned. She had learned to take care of herself very well, and no man would be part of her life again.

She put on her sneakers and her slicker and rain hat and left the boat. She stopped first at MerlInn where Jay was already up and preparing the first of a series of pots of coffee for the guests, none of whom had yet arisen.

She sat behind the counter and, using some of the inn's stationery, wrote out a letter leaving the boat and business to Rico in case she should disappear. She didn't think such a document would stand up in court since she wasn't the legal owner herself, but she didn't think any questions would be asked if he was just to take over. She sealed it in an envelope along with two fifty dollar bills, then wrote his name on top.

Her file envelope was filled with money and she shoved it all into her pockets until they bulged. She was going to have to get herself a purse, something she'd done without for years.

When she was closing up the safe Jay asked her if she was staying for breakfast. She told him she had some shopping to do first but that she'd be back.

She went to her room and hid most of the money beneath her underwear in the drawer, then headed for Duval where the stores were all beginning to open for the day.

Fast Buck's seemed like the best possibility since the other stores carried mostly Key West T-shirts and bikinis. There had been a time when shopping for clothes had been one of the real pleasures in life; now she thought of it as something to get done with as quickly as possible. She no longer even knew what was in style unless what the tourists wore was any indication, and for the most part they seemed to wear as little as possible.

Toby headed for the back of Fast Buck's to look at the clothes and was surprised to see that dresses seemed to have made a comeback. The last time she had gone shopping it was practically all pants and you had to really hunt for a dress. There were still pants, but now there were also racks of dresses and skirts. Linen also seemed to have made a comeback, only this time it came already wrinkled, an innovation that she liked. The trouble with linen had always been that it wrinkled up as soon as you put it on. But if it was supposed to be wrinkled to begin with, that took care neatly of the problem.

The only thing that appealed to her at all was a khaki linen suit and she took it in the dressing room to try on. The skirt was straight and slit to above the knee on one side, and the jacket was an extra long blazer with one button in the front and shoulder pads. Something else she hadn't seen in years.

When she walked out of the dressing room to look at herself in the mirror, the saleswoman came over and showed her how to roll up the sleeves to the elbow for a casual look. She also showed her some blouses that would go with it, and Toby picked up a black cotton shirt blouse with short sleeves.

Another thing that had definitely changed was the price of clothes, but she paid in cash and tried not to think about the dent it put in her savings. She'd need shoes and a bag, but she decided to hit the local shoe stores as the selection at Fast Buck's was slim.

In one store she found a pair of red leather sandals that were flat and seemed comfortable enough, and in another she picked up a pair of red-framed sunglasses that hid half her face. She thought briefly of a hat, but decided it would be a waste of money as she'd never wear it except, perhaps, for the plane trip.

Passing a travel agency, she went inside and purchased a one-way ticket to Miami and another from Miami to New York. She'd have a four-hour layover in Miami, but there was only one flight there a day, and it couldn't be helped.

Her last purchase was a large, canvas tote bag in black that would hold the few belongings she was taking with her. She also purchased a small leather purse to put inside the tote to hold her cash. She was tempted to buy a Key West T-shirt as a souvenir of the place she'd been so happy in, but decided that would be the most foolish thing she could do. It would be like advertising who she was.

At least she wouldn't look out of place arriving in New York with her tan. Not in the middle of the summer. In the winter it might cause comment, but she was sure that even New Yorkers found some sun in the summer months.

The sky looked like it might be starting to clear as she went back to MerlInn and put her new purchases in her room. Toby went over to the dining room where Jay was serving breakfast to several new arrivals, and sat down at one of the tables and helped herself to quiche and a warm bran muffin. The juice was grapefruit, which she didn't care for, but she had a cup of Jay's good coffee.

She would have liked to say good-bye to Jay; wish him well. She even had an urge to tell him her whole story and ask his advice, but she knew the best advice he could give her was what she was planning to do anyway. And she didn't really want to upset him; he was one of the nicest people she knew.

"Fish for dinner tonight?" he asked her.

"It doesn't look like it."

"That's okay. I have steaks in the freezer and I think I'll barbeque tonight if the weather clears. You're invited, of course."

She was beginning to wish her shopping had taken her longer. There was the rest of the day and night to get through before she could leave, and the waiting was already beginning to get to her. She thought of getting a book on New York and reading up on it. But no. After she left, if questions were asked, that would surely be a clue to her whereabouts. On the other hand, she could purchase books about another place, thereby leaving false clues. But she couldn't summon up any interest in reading about another place.

She should have something to read on the plane, though, if for no other reason than to discourage conversation on the part of her seat partner. She went one last time to the book store on Duval, and after perusing the books displayed, finally settled on a science fiction novel, the kind of reading that wouldn't remind her of anything.

The sun was out by that time and Toby decided that rather than spend her last day in town, she'd go out on her boat for one final time of scuba diving. John had taught her, and now, when she had free time, that's what she usually did. She knew it wasn't safe to do alone, that she should have Rico along, but somehow she no longer cared how safe it was. She'd take her chance, tempt fate, as it were.

She saw no signs of activity on Mac's boat as she boarded her own and pulled up the anchor. Good—that way she wouldn't be followed. She had a feeling that if he saw her go out alone he'd think she was making a run for it, and the idea had certainly occurred to her. Only a run to the islands wouldn't be as safe as running away to New York. She was sure all kinds of people successfully eluded being found in that large city, at least she hoped so. It would be a challenge in a way, an adventure. It would be pitting herself against Mac this time rather than her husband, and she thought she could beat him at his own game.

Toby wondered what he'd do when he woke up on Sunday and found her gone. If he even noticed it that soon. He'd check with the airlines, of course, but not knowing the travel agent she dealt with—to whom she had given a phony name—and with all the tourists flying in and out of Key West, she didn't think he'd get on to her very soon. There would be a lot of names he'd have to check out.

Of course, he could discount the couples right away, but still there had to be a lot of single women flying. And the name she had given, Lee Slater, had been ambiguous. If she was lucky, he might think the name belonged to a man. Once in New York and with her newly darkened hair and dark skin, she thought she could successfully blend in with the various ethnic groups of the city. If she was smart, kept her wits about her, she never had to be found again.

At least she fervently hoped so.

Toby was heading out for one of the coral reefs and the sky was growing clearer by the minute. It looked like good weather would prevail for the remainder of the day.

When she reached the point she'd been seeking,

she turned off the engine and went down to drop the anchor off the side. She brought the equipment she'd need to the deck, then stripped off her clothes. She'd need no bathing suit out here where there was no one to see her. Anyway, she loved the feel of the water on her bare skin.

Toby put on the Aqua-Lung, buckling the straps securely in place, then pulling the diving mask over her face she vaulted over the side into the clear water. For a moment she paused to adjust her air supply, then swam down in a long sweeping curve.

The sensation of floating in space, alone in a silent world, never lost its attraction for her. The sunlight, reflected by the waves, shimmered through colorful seagrass which carpeted the bottom and shells and red starfish stood out clearly against the white sand in the clearings.

The reef was a forest of coral twisted into fantastic shapes, ugly, dangerous shapes rising toward the surface like ruined pillars. A few big striped silver perch chased each other through the coral shrubs. She paused, watching them for a moment, and then swam onward with a powerful kick of her webbed feet; fish scattered to avoid her.

Beyond the coral, the bottom vanished from sight as she went over the edge. Down in the depths, shoals of rainbow fish filled the deep blue space, rising and falling in a shimmering cloud, changing color with each movement. They disintegrated in a silver cloud as several blue mackerel burst through them followed by a swordfish.

At that moment, a barracuda flashed from the mist

and poised perhaps twenty feet from her. She watched in stillness as a second later it was joined by another. She couldn't seem to get her fill of seeing them this last time.

When her air supply began to get low, she swam through the shallows above the brilliant red and green color and then the hull of the boat appeared above her and she surfaced astern. She went up the ladder and was about to collapse on the deck when the sight of Mac, replete with swimming trunks, loomed before her.

So he had followed her, she had time to think before he began yelling at her.

"Don't you know how dangerous it is to go diving alone?" His voice sounded as furious as his face looked. He hadn't even seemed to note her naked body in his anger.

She removed her mask and slowly unstrapped the Aqua-Lung. "Danger adds a little spice to it," she answered him flippantly.

He looked like he felt like shaking some sense into her, and she moved back a couple of steps.

"You're a fool, you know it? What do you have, suicidal impulses?"

"I'm alive, aren't I? If I were suicidal, I wouldn't have taken an air supply with me."

He still seemed visibly shaken for some reason. But then she supposed he wouldn't get paid if he returned her to her husband dead. The thought made her angry.

"You need someone to take care of you," he muttered.

"I take care of myself very well, thank you. In fact, I'll probably go down again."

"Over my dead body."

Toby lifted a brow in reply. *Macho, yes. Definitely macho.* "Who appointed you my keeper?" she asked, the sarcasm evident.

He seemed to get himself under control. "All right, so I overreacted. Hell, until I saw the equipment I thought you had drowned. I was about to call the coast guard."

"Mac, I've known you only two days. Before that I was taking care of myself very nicely, and I plan to continue to do so. I'm also a very strong swimmer, and I know this area as well as I know my own boat."

Now his eyes were taking in her body as though gulping air. She stood still for his silent inspection; after all, he'd seen it all before.

"Do you always swim without a suit?"

"When I'm alone, yes. However, if I'd known you were coming...."

Mac grinned. "Don't dress on my account, I like you the way you are."

Toby felt herself growing warm under his gaze and made a move to go past him and down to the cabin to get her clothes. He blocked her and his hands went to her wet breasts, the palms moving lightly across her nipples as she felt them blossom to his touch. She caught her breath as the trembling started. So it wasn't over between them after all. Then, hardly knowing what she had in mind, she moved from him and dove over the side of the boat, surfacing several yards away.

He had followed her in.

She swam away from the boat, then treaded water while he caught up to her. He was a good swimmer, but not as strong as she. Once beside her in the water, she caught the gleam in his eyes and tried to evade the arms that were closing around her, but she didn't move fast enough and the next thing she knew he was pulling them both under. When she emerged again she was spitting water.

"Despite your fantasies to the contrary, it really isn't possible in the water," she told him, feeling playful for no discernible reason.

"No fantasy, it's just that we both happen to be in the water."

Toby gave him a look of mock pity. "No fantasies? Poor man. What would life be without fantasies?" She paddled around him, not trying to get out of his reach as she knew he was really helpless to do anything. As far as that went, she didn't really care if he did. The sight of his nearly naked body in the clear water was turning her on.

Mac grinned at her. "Why indulge in fantasies when you can have the real thing?" He made a sudden lunge for her, but she evaded him and he went under again while she watched laughing.

"Sometimes fantasies are safer," she said.

"I'm sure they're always safer, just not as satisfying. Anyway, who wants to be safe?"

She felt her smile falter. *I'd settle for safe,* she thought, *yes, indeed, I would.* She poised, then dove deeper into the water, not coming up this time until his hands were on her body and she felt herself beginning not to care whether she drowned. There was something extremely sensuous about his hands on her wet body. She thought if they both had diving gear on she'd give it a try, but she didn't and their play was becoming dangerous.

She headed for the boat, swimming fast, then scrambled up the rope ladder. He was still in the water and she went below, then quickly returned to the deck with a towel wrapped around her sarong style.

He was standing there, the water running off his smooth body, his hair appealingly covering his forehead. Toby felt a rush of affection for him and wanted to play with him as children play, but the look in his eyes was anything but childish.

"You don't need that," he said of the towel.

Her eyes traveled halfway down his body. "Nor do you need that," she said of his trunks, "or did you think they were sexy?" Which, in fact, they were—very brief and very tight, the kind of suit that made you wonder why the wearer bothered with it at all.

When he seemed to hesitate, she opened up the towel and held it wide, offering him her body. He quickly removed his trunks and moved in next to her and she lifted her mouth to meet his.

She let the towel drop to the deck as an electrical charge surged through her at his touch. His kiss was demanding, as were his hands and his body, and she started lowering herself to the deck, pulling him down on top of her. She didn't care that it wasn't as comfortable as her bunk; she had always wondered what it would be like to make love on the deck in the open air, beneath the sun. It actually was one of her fantasies.

Just the enveloping touch of him in the breathless, muggy world was better than any of her fantasies had been. With shiftings of her body and movements with her hands, she was able to direct him in what she wanted, and she felt a surge of power that she could bend him to her own pleasure so easily. It was a new feeling, having power in sex, and she reveled in it.

But there came a moment when foreplay would no longer suffice, when she wanted him inside of her so badly she thought she would scream. She positioned her body and began to move her hips, letting him know what she wanted, and he rose above her briefly before entering her with a sharp thrust. The pleasure was so total she gasped, her legs winding strongly around his body and pulling him even deeper inside her until a pleasurable pain evolved into ecstasy.

Toby was aware of the hard deck beneath her and the way Mac's movements corresponded with the rocking of the boat. Her eyes closed against the glaring sun, she met each movement with one of her own so that their wet bodies were slapping against each other with hurricane force. It wasn't sweet, slow, gentle sex, but she found it far more exciting and felt she could go on forever.

He was finished slightly before she, and Toby opened her eyes when she felt the explosion building inside her and watched him as he watched her come to her own powerful conclusion.

Afterward she pushed him off and spread her body to face the sun. She didn't feel the need for kisses or endearments or whatever was to follow. She wanted to hug the moment to herself, to go over every detail and etch it into her mind, so that she had it to remember when a need for fantasies was with her once again. She felt replete in a way that had nothing to do with him and any interference on his part, at this point, would only diminish that feeling.

Her power didn't seem to be absolute, though, because he was now up on one elbow and smiling down at her and she knew the lovely silence was about to be broken.

"Was I there for you at all?" he was asking.

"What?"

"I had the feeling I was just a tool, that you were using me."

Toby didn't feel inclined to deny it. After all, he was the one she was forced to escape from, wasn't he? "Haven't you ever used a woman?"

Mac sank back on the deck, his eyes not meeting hers. "I suppose so."

"Probably often, am I right?"

He was silent for a long moment. "I wasn't using you."

"What would you call it then?"

"I would call it making love."

A laugh escaped her. "I think that had very little to do with love. Look, I'm not complaining."

"I know you're not; that's what bothers me."

She reached for the towel she had earlier discarded and folded it to put it beneath her head. The sun on her body felt wonderful and she wondered if she'd ever sunbathe again.

"I think we should talk, Toby."

"We have nothing to talk about, Mac. Ships in the night, remember?"

"I think it's gone beyond that." ·

She gave him a look of surprise and saw that he was serious. "Ready to sail off into the sunset with me? Is that it?" She couldn't help the playful tone, there was no way she was going to take him seriously.

His eyes were closed now against the sun. "You make me feel things I haven't felt in a long time."

"How long? Since the beginning of your current affair? Well, you said that was about over. You'll find someone else and get those feelings back again."

"No, longer than that. You make me feel the way I felt when I was young and still hopeful about men and women getting together. When I still had illusions, I guess."

She propped herself up on one elbow and stared down at him. She didn't want to hear him baring his soul; she had enough problems of her own. "And that's all it is, Mac, an illusion. Don't get carried away by an illusion. Illusions are ephemeral at best."

"Am I hearing the charter boat captain as philosopher?"

"You're hearing some common sense, that's all."

"What's common sense got to do with this? If it did, we wouldn't even be here together."

She couldn't argue with that. Common sense, in fact, was telling her to get rid of him now. "I'm not sure why we even are together, Mac. Are you?" Keep him on the defensive. Let him answer his own questions. She was almost free of him, she assuredly wasn't going to slip up now.

"I don't know," it almost sounded like a grumble.

"I'm beginning to think it's fate. Or someone up there's playing a practical joke on me."

She laughed out loud, and he turned to her in annoyance. "All right, I know how ridiculous that sounds. What's the mystery, anyway. A man and a woman are attracted, what's unusual about that?"

"Don't ask me—you're the one who started this."

"It's just that I think I'm more than attracted."

"Believe me, you're not."

"Don't tell me what I'm feeling. Don't you think I'd like it to be only an attraction? Or even less?"

If Mac was about to come out with a declaration of love she was going to shove him over the side of the boat. Would this man stop at nothing to entrap her? "I think you're using a well-worn line on me, Mac, and it's not taking."

"You're just so innately suspicious of men you don't know sincerity when you hear it."

Toby stopped the laugh that was bubbling up inside her. If this man had been sincere with her even for a second, she'd eat her hat. The yellow one that went with her slicker.

"Who said I was innately suspicious of men? Maybe I just don't like them."

"Are you telling me you don't like me?"

"I'm not telling you anything—I'm just offering possibilities." Toby was trying desperately to maintain this conversation on a light note, but he wasn't helping any.

"You might be managing to fool yourself, but you're not fooling me. Whatever there is between us, it's strong and it's mutual."

"Come on, Mac, are you trying to tell me every encounter is mutual?"

"This one is. Do you want me to prove it?" Without waiting for an answer, his hand went to one of her breasts and she felt herself dissolving against the deck.

"That's just sex."

His hand began to caress her. "Just sex? You think sex is something impersonal like eating or drinking?"

"I think it's relatively unimportant against the larger picture," she said, getting to her feet and once more diving over the side of the boat. She didn't want his hand on her again, and she certainly didn't want an in-depth conversation on sex. This was her last day on the boat and she wanted it as uncomplicated as possible.

Of course he jumped in after her, and she only hoped it would cool him off. Cool them both off. Not too easy in water that was probably eighty-five degrees, but it was a lot cooler than the air temperature. Toby swam over to the ladder and stood on the first rung, then turned around so that her back was to the boat and steadied herself by holding the sides of the rope. She suddenly felt very, very good, on top of everything. Maybe the man really was torn between his duty and his desire. Good, she hoped he was. It would serve him right. Private detectives, in all probability, never felt such pangs of conscience. Might even make him think about going into a different line of work.

Mac swam up to her and grabbed hold of the ropes

so that their bodies were inches apart, half submerged
and half out of the water. He was below her on the
ladder so that they were eye level and she couldn't
keep the feeling of power out of her eyes.

He didn't question it though, and she felt a sudden
loss of power as his lips met hers and their bodies
pressed together. She felt a loss of control, but at the
moment didn't care. The sex with him was so inexpli-
cably good that she couldn't seem to get enough of it.
Thank God she was leaving tomorrow; a week of this
and she didn't think she'd be able to leave. Maybe it
was mutual; maybe he was having the same thoughts.
After all, what he was doing couldn't really be faked.
Men were at a disadvantage that way.

He moved down a rung on the ladder so that his
face was between her breasts; and his mouth began to
move over them. She wondered if they tasted of salt
water, and felt one hand go around to press his face in
closer to her. She'd like to own him, is what she'd
like. She'd like to have a cage installed on her boat
and keep him there, bringing him out when the need
arose, letting him fulfill those needs and then locking
him back up in his cage. And in that moment of thinking, and with a sense of horror, she suddenly understood her husband very well. In essence, that's what
he had done to her, wasn't it? Dear God, was she as
perverted as he?

Toby felt shaken at the thought and barely noticed
the things that Mac was doing to her body. Oh, her
body was responding all right, but her mind was
locked into her new thoughts, and she was dismayed
at what they revealed. Would she really want to keep

Mac in a cage? Away from other women? Away from all temptation? Or did she subconsciously just want to keep him from doing his job? She had to admit that the job had nothing to do with it at all and she shuddered at the thought.

What it amounted to was she wanted to own another human being, much as her husband had owned her. Had he poisoned her in some way so that she had become like him, or did this feeling exist to some degree in all people?

She moaned, letting go of the rope, but Mac's body held her in place and she didn't fall. "Oh, God, I don't believe this," she cried out, her emotions in a tumult.

"Believe it," Mac murmured, obviously thinking her overcome with passion.

"No," she said, pushing his head away, not wanting to use him when her thoughts were anywhere but on sex, or at least the sex that was now being offered up.

He moved up a rung and crushed her in his arms. "Don't fight it, Toby," he said, then covered her mouth with his own. His feelings seemed to enter into her, and she felt herself being taken over by what he wanted—what she now wanted too. He entered her beneath the water, which made it tight at first, but then she relaxed and it began to feel like the only thing in the world that really mattered. All thought fled from her mind leaving only desire and something else, something nameless.

They made love slowly, their mouths never parting, and she felt herself reaching the peak and then dropping over not once, not twice, but in a succession of moments that left her, finally, stunned and shaken.

"You're incredible," he murmured to her at one point, but it wasn't she who was incredible, it was what he was doing to her.

She was left so weak that he had to help her up onto the deck where he held her as she collapsed into his arms.

"What am I going to do with you, Toby?" Mac asked at last, his own voice sounding shaken.

"I don't know—what are you going to do with me?" she said, daring him to tell her the truth at that moment.

But all he said was, "I don't know. I just don't know."

She followed him back to Garrison Bight and moored beside him, both of them dropping anchor at the same time. She'd agreed to have dinner with him and really saw no harm in it. She had to eat, didn't she, and there was the long evening to get through with nothing on her mind but leaving the following morning. And let him buy her a good dinner; that way she'd have more money to take with her to New York.

As she dressed in clean shorts and T-shirt she had an unaccountable desire to go into town and put on her new clothes—let him see her looking smart for once. But of course that wouldn't do at all. Anyway, was she trying to impress him? Did she even need to impress him at this point?

He, as usual, emerged from his cabin looking like a man in a cologne ad but he seemed less at ease in his clothes than she did in hers. Or maybe she was just imagining it.

"You pick out the restaurant," he told her. "You know this place better than I do."

She took him to *Chez Emile* on Front Street. Toby had always longed to eat there but couldn't justify the price of the food to herself. Let him worry about it. It would probably go on an expense account that her husband would ultimately pay, anyway. Although her husband, she had to admit, had never been cheap about food. But then he had the money to be extravagant.

It was early yet and not crowded, and they were led to a table overlooking the water. There was a candle on the table and a single rose, and soft music was playing in the background. Altogether romantic, she thought, and altogether wasted on them.

They both ordered steaks and salads and fresh asparagus in addition to a carafe of wine, and once again she wished she were wearing her new suit. The people dining at *Chez Emile* were dressed better than the usual tourists she saw on the street. But Mac's eyes were looking at her in a way that made her feel like the best dressed woman in the room.

Mac lit a cigarette without even checking his watch and she realized she hadn't seen him smoke in hours. "You're doing pretty good with that, aren't you?" she asked him, her eyes going to his cigarette.

"Somehow, with you, I forget about smoking."

"Probably because your hands are busy elsewhere," she couldn't resist saying, and saw his answering smile.

"I think you're some kind of sea sprite out to bewitch me," he said.

Toby grinned at him. "You writers do get fanciful," she said with a southern accent.

"There's nothing more prosaic than a travel writer," Mac countered, and they were back once again to lying to each other. She didn't mind; lies were safer by far. She had to counter the tendency she thought she saw in him to level with her. The last thing she wanted to hear was what he really did for a living. That would make for a confrontation, some kind of resolution. She had to avoid that for at least several more hours.

"So tell me about your travels."

"That's like asking you to tell me about the biggest fish you've caught."

"Oh, we fishermen are always eager to talk about that," she told him, which had its basis in truth. She could regale him with fish stories all evening if that's what he wanted.

"No, tell me something else," he said. "If we were to sail off into the sunset together, where would you want to go?"

"Do you know where Belize is?"

"Of course. We travel writers get around, you know."

"There are islands off Belize—I've heard they're like paradise. Have you ever been there?"

"No, but I've been in that area. You like the tropics, don't you?"

"If you had grown up in Michigan, you'd like

them, too." She was hoping she got that right. It was Michigan she had told him, wasn't it?

It seemed to be because he didn't question it. "So what would you do on this romantic island of yours?"

"Did I say it was romantic?"

"If we were there together it would be."

"Fish, scuba dive, sunbathe. What else is there?"

"You can do all that here."

"I know; I do."

"Then why your urge to leave the country?"

She hesitated. "No real urge. This is fantasy time, remember?"

"Would your boat make it there?"

Toby shrugged. "I have no idea, but yours would."

The waiter placed their salads in front of them, and all conversation ceased for the moment. John had told her about the islands off Belize. One in particular, but she couldn't remember the name of it. He had made it sound like perfection, particularly the part about very few tourists, and once in a while in her daydreams she'd think about it. But not having any identification papers, it had never been a real possibility. If she were free, though, and could go anywhere....

"You're a million miles away," Mac was saying to her.

She looked up at him and smiled. "No, only as far as Belize."

"You really want to go there, don't you?"

"Sometimes I get the urge."

"And what do you do to quell that urge?"

"I don't. It just remains."

"What if I said, let's leave tonight?"

Toby turned from him angrily. "More supposition. Why don't you say, let's leave?"

"Is that what you want me to say?"

"I'd like to hear you say something real just once!"

They looked at each other in shocked silence for a minute, neither willing to say the next word. They were saved by the waiter bringing their entree, and they both subsided into eating. The quiet music in the background suddenly seemed very loud.

The steak was rare and tender, just the way she liked it, but Toby barely tasted it. She had almost forced him into saying something she really didn't want to hear, and she was unnerved by her own actions. *Watch it*, she warned herself; *just spend the rest of the evening making polite conversation and don't rock the boat.*

When she reached to pour herself some more wine, his eyes caught hers. "Better be careful of that stuff, you might talk too much."

And just what did he mean by that? "What about you? I don't see you drinking your designer water tonight."

He choked on his food and had to revive himself with some water. "What have you got against Perrier?"

"Aside from the pretentious name and the more pretentious price?"

Mac laughed at that. "Perhaps I move in pretentious circles."

Perhaps, but she didn't think so. Despite the clothes and the boat and the water, she had a feeling he didn't move in pretentious circles at all.

"Is there somewhere in town we could go to dance?" he asked.

"I don't want to dance."

"Come on, you can't be afraid to be close to me. Not now."

"I'm not dressed for dancing. Unless you have in mind one of those discotheques the college kids go to."

"No, that wasn't what I had in mind." But he dropped it, probably in deference to how she was dressed.

The waiter came by to see if they wanted dessert. Mac ordered coffee and a brandy and Toby asked for tea and chocolate mousse. Might as well indulge while she could.

When they left the restaurant he took her hand and started off in the direction of the marina. She stopped in the middle of the sidewalk and let go of his hand. "I'll say goodnight to you here, Mac. I'm going to spend the night in town." She had an urge to hug him to her, to say good-bye.

He seemed to be about to argue, then thought better of it. "You want me to walk you where you're going?"

"No, it's only a few blocks. Thanks for the dinner, it was really nice."

"Will I see you tomorrow?"

"Not if the weather holds. I do have to make a living, you know."

He drew her into his arms and kissed her softly on the lips. "Maybe we can get together tomorrow night, then."

"Sure," she lied. "I'd like that."

Toby had to hold together her exposed nerves very tightly then and force back the tears that seemed to be forming behind her eyes. It was the last time she would ever see him, and somehow that knowledge didn't make her as happy as she had expected it would.

Somehow she didn't feel very happy at all.

Chapter Eight

The alarm woke him up. He hadn't wanted to take any chances of missing his plane, not with his usual proclivity for sleep. Not that he'd slept all that well, and that damned Toby was responsible for that.

Mac reached for a cigarette and lit it, shoving his pillow up on the wall behind his head. He had a problem. A big problem. And he didn't know what to do about it. How had a guy who'd been married twice, both times disastrously, and who was now gun-shy of women as far as emotional involvements were concerned, get so emotionally involved with a woman so damned fast? He wasn't going to use the word love; he'd be damned if he'd use that word, but his emotions were involved to the point that he was thinking about her constantly and very little about the job at hand. And the fact that they were interconnected just made it worse.

Hell, what he'd really like to do was run away with her, and he found himself wondering if she'd really be willing. He had a feeling she might be, and that feeling was driving him to distraction. He'd lain awake half the night fantasizing—yes, fantasizing!—about just such a possibility. Quitting his job, throwing it all over, and taking off with her. And it wasn't just the sex, although that was a large part of it. It was also her. Toby wasn't the most stimulating conversationalist he'd ever encountered, but he had a feeling that was due to the fact that they were both lying to each other. He could do better himself when he wasn't having to watch every word he said. And there was something about her that told him he'd never find her boring. And if that were true, she was one in a million and he didn't want to let her go.

Hell, he was hooked. Came down to do a simple little job, and look where he wound up. Hooked! He wasn't even thinking like an adult anymore; he was thinking like a little kid who wants his candy and wants to eat it, too. And speaking of wants, what he also wanted was a cup of coffee.

Mac got out of bed and went to the galley. Out the window he saw Toby's boat still moored beside his although the sun was out and there was nary a cloud in the sky. Had the charterers cancelled out? He was going to take care of a little business in Miami, and then when he came back to her he was going to persuade her to sail off into the sunset with him. At least that had been the decision he had come to shortly before dawn.

What if she said no? *Would* she say no? If he had the goods on her, how *could* she say no? So she'd enjoyed the adventure, liked the extra money. So what. She'd also enjoyed him, he was confident of it, and when she learned her smuggling days were over anyway, why wouldn't she agree? He knew if he could get her alone with him for any length of time she'd never leave him. Maybe that was supreme ego on his part, but he didn't think so. He thought she felt the same way he felt, and if that was truly the case she wouldn't want to leave him any more than he wanted to leave her.

Was this actually Mac McTaggert having these thoughts? The Mac who these days successfully evaded all attempts by women to pin him down? Well, no one ever said it had to last forever, but while it did. . . .

He stirred the instant coffee into the cup of boiled water and wondered if he was having a nervous breakdown. Surely what he intended to do went against everything he believed in. But maybe it was his beliefs that needed reassessment, not his desires.

Maybe she really didn't give a damn. Maybe she was on to him and just playing him for a fool. And maybe she'd just been faking all those responses of hers, but he didn't think so. He didn't think any woman was that good a fake, and he'd sure met plenty who tried.

And maybe he did need a day away from her to try to get his head straightened out!

He showered, then dressed in yet another designer delight. The clothes didn't even bother him much anymore. He was changing in more ways than one, and he didn't know what to do about it.

Was Toby a bleached blonde? Wasn't she? Did blondes have more fun? *Were* blondes more fun? Was he on his way to ending up on the funny farm?

He didn't know. He didn't seem to know anything for sure anymore. Maybe he'd go back to the booze; at least that had always seemed to answer all his questions at the time. But not now. Right now he had to get to Miami and settle a few things.

He took a taxi to the airport and was sitting in the lounge waiting for the boarding call to be announced when he spotted her. At first he thought he truly was going nuts, that he was fantasizing her. For one thing she was dressed in a suit, and that was more like he'd fantasize her than how she'd actually dress. He thought, *You're crazy, Mac, it's just another blonde*, but then as she moved closer into his view he knew without a doubt that it was her, knew without a doubt that he was as sane as the next man and what he saw wasn't a figment of his imagination. He could even tell she wasn't wearing a bra under that black blouse of hers.

He stood up and was starting to call out her name when she saw him, and if he'd had doubts before they would have vanished then at the look of recognition and shock on her face. Before he could say anything, she turned and practically ran into the ladies' room, and that was that.

What the hell was she doing at the airport? Well, thinking constructively there were two possibilities. One, she was meeting someone on the Miami flight, and two, she was going to Miami herself. If she was meeting someone, he'd like to stick around and see who, but he had to be on that flight himself. If she was catching the flight, he'd corner her on board and find out just what was up. Because something was up.

The last he heard she was taking out charterers today. And it wasn't a plane they were going to fish from.

When the flight was called, Toby still hadn't reappeared out of the ladies' room, and he knew because he hadn't taken his eyes from it. Anyone watching him would have taken him for some kind of voyeur. Mac waited until everyone else had boarded, then got on the plane and watched the exit to see if she would arrive late. When she didn't, and they finally took off, he wasted no time in ordering a drink. He needed it.

Well, this was one little mystery he wasn't going to be able to solve until he returned to Key West. But if it had anything to do with her going to Miami or meeting anyone from Miami, then it had to be drug related. Not that he'd really had any hopes it was otherwise. Everything fitted in too perfectly.

What was that she had been carrying? A large canvas bag, that's what. And just why would she be carrying a large canvas bag unless she were either going somewhere or delivering something. How much cocaine would a bag that size hold? Enough, brother.

The flight attendant went by and he caught her attention and ordered another drink. She gave him a friendly smile, the kind he'd usually take as a come-on, but this time he wasn't even interested. She could have black hair and brown eyes and be built like Sophia Loren for all he cared, he just wasn't interested. At the moment, there was a small blonde who was filling up all the recesses of his mind.

He carried on arguments with himself all the way to Miami, but it was a short trip and he'd solved nothing by the time he got there. He didn't see Boogie around:

not when he disembarked, not by the information counter, and not in the bar where Mac stopped for another quick drink. After all, he was going to need it, wasn't he?

Mac went over to one of the public wall phones and called his office. He got the duty officer, who told him the message from Boogie was that he'd meet him in their usual place that night at eight. Their usual place meant a bar and eight meant that he wouldn't get the afternoon flight back to Key West. He went over to the airline counter and changed his afternoon flight for one on Monday morning. So he'd miss seeing Toby tonight. By tomorrow he'd at least have everything settled once and for all.

Not wanting to bother stopping by his place first, he rented a car and drove to Palm Beach where he figured his boss would be either at home or on the golf course. The one thing George liked, as well as nabbing cocaine smugglers, was shooting under par, and he had a good reputation for both.

He found him at home where George's wife gave him a less than welcoming nod, before sending him back to the patio where his boss was lying in a hammock and listening to a ball game on a portable radio set up next to him. Also next to him was a long, cool drink, and Mac found himself accepting the offer of one of his own.

"I want to talk to you, George."

"Of course you do. That's why you're here. Not about Boogie, is it? I understood you were to see him tonight?"

"No, not about Boogie."

"So how's Key West? Enjoying yourself down there? I always liked it there, nice place to retire. Of course it's gotten awfully gay, but then they're coming out of the woodwork here, too. Even letting them in the agency now, you hear about that?"

Mac let him run on until his drink arrived and George's wife once again departed. Then, "I want to be taken off the case."

George's head peered up over the side of the hammock. "Did I hear you right? Taken off?"

"I'm afraid I've become personally involved." *And what's more, George, I want to run away with the suspect.* He felt like saying it, but had the good sense not to.

"Better tell me about it, Mac."

"I just told you. I've become personally involved with the suspect."

"Well, good for you—that's part of the job."

Mac sat down in one of the white wrought iron chairs, put his drink down on a table, and rested his elbows on his knees. Covering his eyes, he said, "I wouldn't go so far as to say I'm in love with her, George, but—"

"In love? Is that what you said? I thought it was a man you were investigating down there. You did say her, didn't you?"

"It turned out to be a woman. The man died and she took over for him is the way I see it. No, George, I've not come out of the closet." *Worse—I've gone over to the side of the enemy,* Mac thought to himself.

George was obviously so affected by this piece of information that he got out of the hammock and sat in a chair facing Mac. He wasn't even listening to the ball game anymore. "So what do you want, Mac, a deal for her? If she cooperates, we can arrange something, you know that."

"I just want to take her out of there—somewhere safe. Hell, George, I'm not sure what I want. I'm not so deranged that I want to foul up the job. Just take me off the job and let someone else do the dirty work."

"You think that'll endear you to her? Incidentally, what happened to Maria? One in every port?" He chuckled and Mac winced at the sound.

"I just thought I'd tell you, that's all. The way I feel now I don't think I could do the job."

"Then turn her."

"What?"

"You heard me, turn her. Get her to work for us. She's perfectly placed, already knows the ins and outs, obviously has no record. That's the ticket, Mac—turn her."

"I don't know if she'd go for it."

"Wouldn't you if the DEA was on to you? Look, what's she in it for? Money? We can pay her. Adventure? Hell, we're as adventurous as they are. Turn her and you can go on loving her with a clear conscience."

Mac was feeling the effects of the latest in a series of drinks. "I think you may have something there, George."

"Sure I do. Solved all your problems in one fell swoop, didn't I? Except maybe the problem of Maria, but I'm sure you can handle that."

Maria seemed to be the least of his problems at the

moment. "We could work together," he said, doing his thinking out loud. "The two of us would be a team."

"For a while, yes. But I don't expect Key West to remain a problem for long."

"And after Key West? Would you still keep her on?"

"I'm sure there's always a place in the DEA for a woman of her talents."

"I don't think she'd like Miami."

"What's the matter with Miami?" asked George, obviously forgetting he lived in Palm Beach, which was a whole lot different than Miami.

"So I have your authorization for this?"

"Hell, yes you have my authorization. Wasn't it my idea? Go to it, Mac. Give her the speech about helping her country in its moment of anguish—"

"What moment of anguish?"

"You know what I mean. Come across as the hero, fighting the forces of evil."

"I think you watch too much television, George."

"Can't even listen to a ball game around here. And on my day off, too."

Mac stood up and smiled down at him. "Listen to your ball game, George—I'll be in touch."

"Let me know right away what she says."

Mac nodded, then headed around the house to the driveway where the rented Ford was parked. Why hadn't he thought of it himself? It was perfect. He was sure she'd go for it, sure she'd take the way out that he was offering her. And without denying her spirit of adventure, too. And the two of them would work great together. They wouldn't have to do something stupid like getting married, of course. Just work together. And occasionally play together. Just the thought of it warmed his soul.

His soul froze up again quickly when he reached home and saw Maria's Jaguar parked in front of the complex that housed his condo. She wasn't inside, so he took the time to get out of his costume and into some regular clothes, then fixed himself a drink. He looked down out of the window in his kitchen and saw her spread out in the sun beside the pool wearing her latest: a string bikini that covered about four square inches of her body.

He wasn't the only one looking at her. Practically every single man in the building, and a few of the marrieds, were sunbathing in her general vicinity, all with an eye cocked in her direction. He figured they were waiting for her to move to see if the suit fell off.

He went down the outside stairs to the pool area and drew up a chair beside her. "Looking good, Maria."

"Where you been, Mac? You just go off without even telling me? What do you think, I don't worry?"

Would someone worried think about sunbathing? "Work, babe, you know how it is."

"Yes, I know how it is. I know too well how it is." The neighbors were now not only enjoying the string bikini, they were also enjoying the heated conversation.

"Let's go inside, Maria."

"What for? This is the first time the sun's been out in days. Hey, Mac, you want to see my tan?"

He thought he could already see it, but she was pulling one of the small triangles over that covered one breast and giving him and a few others a view of lighter skin and brown nipple. Mac found himself averting his eyes, which did not go unnoticed by Maria.

"What's the matter, you don't like a peek? Huh? Everyone else likes a peek, but not you, Mac?"

"Couldn't we go inside, Maria? Please? I can't stay long—"

"You running off again? You're not even spending the night? You think I like spending nights alone, Mac?"

Mac could count several men who'd be glad to take his place, all of them honing in on every word now.

"You know how my job is. It's been the same way ever since we met."

"I didn't like it then, either."

He sighed and got up. "I'll be inside for a while if you want to talk."

He knew it would work and it did. She got up and followed him, leaving a hushed silence in her wake.

Once inside, though, she headed straight for the bedroom and he knew he was in trouble. Maria liked to fight and make up, and she must have considered their brief argument outside to be a fight. Which meant that he was going to be expected to make up. He really didn't think he was going to be up for that.

By the time he had followed her into the bedroom, her string bikini was off and looking like a used tissue on the floor. Maria—hips swaying, eyelashes batting provocatively, mouth being wetted down by her tongue—was moving toward him and it didn't look like she had talking on her mind.

He edged into the room and slid into the chair usually only used when he put on his shoes and socks. "Sit down, Maria; I really think we ought to talk."

"Later we talk," she murmured, coming over to him and starting to undo the buttons of his shirt. Her mouth began to blow softly in his ear as her hands explored downward.

"What's the matter with you, Mac? You're not even excited."

She seemed excited enough for both of them. "Look, we really need to talk." He was beginning to sound like a broken record.

She settled down on his lap, her arms around his neck and the tips of her lush breasts crushed provocatively against his chest. "Okay, talk!"

It would have been easier to just have one last time with her. He couldn't even think of what to say. The really surprising part was that he felt no desire for her at all anymore, and that had been the best thing she had going for her. He certainly hadn't liked her for her mental stimulation.

"I . . . I feel rotten having to tell you this, babe, but I met someone else."

"You what?" Her eyes flew open and her Cuban accent came to the fore.

"It wasn't intentional, it just happened."

"You and another woman?" She seemed to grasp that much, at least.

"It started off as business, I swear, but then . . ." he spread his hands in a hopeless gesture.

"You been seeing another woman behind my back?"

He nodded his head.

She started to laugh, a raucous sound that filled the room. Pretty soon she was shaking in his lap and tears were streaming down her face. He had an urge to join in the laughter but didn't know why. He also didn't feel it would be right. After all, it might not be real laughter; it might be hysteria.

It wasn't. "That is the funniest thing I ever heard, Mac, you know that? You been seeing another woman, I been seeing another man."

He felt a surge of relief at her words before they fully penetrated and he felt some stirrings of jealousy. "You've been seeing another man behind my back?"

"Yes, for several weeks now," she said between her laughs.

"Several *weeks*? Thanks a lot, Maria!"

"What's the matter with you? It works out perfectly, no? You have your new woman, I have my new man. We should have a drink and celebrate."

Yeah, perfect. And here he thought he was going to break her heart. Some heart!

"Hey, you want to do it once more for old time's sake, Mac? How about it, I already have my clothes off anyway."

He pushed her off his lap and stood up. "No thanks."

"Hey, you mad at me? I'm not mad at you."

"Why should you be? You cheated first." Even as he said them he knew how childish the words sounded. Oh, hell, maybe it was all the drinks. He got out of a tight situation with no sweat. What did he have to bitch about?

"Thanks, Maria, but it wouldn't feel right." Noble now, that's what he was. Or maybe he just didn't think he'd be able to manage it with all the booze in him.

"I already moved my clothes out," she said, getting into her minute bathing suit again. "I was going to leave you a note when I left today."

"A note? You were going to leave me a note?"

"Well, what do you expect? Did you tell me where you were going? Did you even tell me that you were going? It would have been a nice note. A little sad, but nice."

He reached out his arms to her and she ran into them. "It's been good, Maria."

"Yes, it was always good. When you were around, which wasn't a lot of the time, Mac."

"I know. Good luck with your new one. I hope he sticks around more."

"Oh, yes. He owns a restaurant. I know where he is all the time."

He walked her to the door, kissed her good-bye, then, on the way to the bar, decided he didn't need another drink. He had a few hours to kill so he went outside and swam a few lengths of the pool. The water reminded him of Toby, but that was all right. He liked being reminded of Toby.

He only hoped she went for his proposition. On the other hand, what real choice did she have? If the DEA was on to her she couldn't very well maintain business as usual. He was sure she would go for it, and it would be a hell of a lot of fun working with her. And when they weren't working—that would be even more fun.

He went inside, set his alarm clock, then stretched out on his bed for a nap. Now, with all his problems solved, he ought to be able to sleep like a baby.

Boogie wasn't in the bar yet when he arrived. He ordered a beer, even made it a light, then lit a cigarette and looked around. The usual sleazy crowd, but no one into anything really big. Two of the resident hookers were eyeing him, but they'd both met up with Maria and he thought they'd keep their distance. And that was really a change, wanting women to keep their distance. Not only was he going to reform Toby, but he was reforming.

Mac wished he could call her just to hear her voice, but her not having a phone took care of that. Maybe he could try the MerlInn? No, he'd wait until tomorrow. Anyway, there was nothing he could really say to her over the phone, it would have to be in person. But what the hell had she been doing at the airport? And dressed up? She didn't bother dressing up for him. And maybe he shouldn't even think about getting mad at her until he found out her reasons.

The beer came and he drank half of it down. The effects of the former drinks had dissipated with his sleep, but he now had a hell of a thirst. Toby. Those large eyes that were so dark a blue they almost seemed black at times. That cute little nose, that soft mouth, that body that could drive him wild. God, he wished he could be with her tonight. But there'd be tomorrow night and all the other nights as long as it lasted. And how could it not last? They were dynamite together.

Boogie boogied through the door and waved a few greetings before sidling over to Mac at the bar. "I'll have my usual," he said to the bartender, and was given a Pepsi Light. Big drinker, Boogie.

"I hear you've been trying to reach me," said Mac, but Boogie was not one to be hurried.

"You want to hear how I did today, Mac?" he asked, then answered him anyway by telling him about every race he'd bet on and whether he won or lost. It could have been Greek for all Mac knew about horse racing.

"So, did you come out ahead?"

"I just told you, didn't I?" Boogie looked affronted.

"Sorry, Boogie, I got things on my mind."

"Hey, Mac, you want to hit a disco tonight? New one I think you'd like, mostly Cuban."

Boogie knew his liking for Latin women. Well, his former liking. Right now he was into blondes.

"Not tonight, Boogie. I need my sleep."

"You mean Maria's waiting for you."

He didn't disabuse Boogie of the notion. "So what have you got for me, Boogie?"

"This is good stuff, Mac—gonna cost you."

"How much?"

"Coupla hundred?" Boogie's eyes were manic in their eagerness.

"Let's hear it."

Boogie moved in closer and practically whispered in his ear. "The way I hear it it's on for Tuesday night."

"Good source?"

"The best."

"This coming Tuesday?"

"You got it!"

Mac reached for his wallet and pulled out two bills. "Thanks, Boogie—if it works out I'll have another hundred for you."

Boogie shoved the money in his pants pocket and began to look shiftily around the room. "Got to boogie, Mac," he said, moving off.

"See you," said Mac.

Mac finished his beer and then headed back to his condo. He'd watch a little TV, then hit the sack early. He was going to have a big day tomorrow.

Before going to bed he took out a canvas flight bag and packed some of his own clothes. He was damned if he was going to spend the remainder of his time in Key West in those foolish looking Ralph Lauren clothes he had bought.

Chapter Nine

Rico banged on the door to her room shortly after dawn on Sunday and Toby woke with a start. The room was pitch dark and for a moment she couldn't remember what day it was. She turned on the bedside lamp and saw her new suit hanging from the knob on the door to the wardrobe, and what she was going to do today came flooding back to her.

The banging continued and she could hear Rico's voice whispering her name.

She opened the door and stuck her head out. "I'm going to have to cancel today, Rico—I think I have a stomach flu." Another lie in a long series of lies.

"Hey, Toby, you okay?"

"I'll survive."

"I was worried, you know?"

"You're going to have to tell the men, I don't want you taking them out alone."

"Don't worry about them, Toby, I already fixed it up so they would go out with Willie. He had a party cancel out."

"Good. Thanks."

"How come you're sick, Toby? You've never been sick before."

"I don't know—I think it must have been something I ate."

"I was worried after what you said yesterday. About if something happened to you, you know?"

"I'll be fine tomorrow, I promise." She hated lying to him more than she'd ever hated lying to anyone. Children were always getting lied to, it seemed, and it didn't seem fair.

He looked her face over carefully, then nodded, as though reassuring himself that she didn't look like she was going to die. "Okay, see you tomorrow then."

"Thanks again, Rico."

It was no use going back to bed because she'd never get back to sleep. Which meant that now she had several hours to kill before going to the airport. She decided to use part of the time to wash the dark roots out of her hair. Mac had known who she was despite the roots, and just once she'd like to look less cheap and more herself. By tomorrow at this time she would be a brunette, anyway.

It usually took about a dozen shampoos before the dye disappeared, and she got under the shower and hoped the hot water would hold up for that many washings. She had some liquid detergent left from doing her laundry and washed it the first two times with that. It was much stronger than her shampoo, and with only two additional washings the roots came out looking the same color as her hair. Then she put some conditioner on it, something she usually neglected to do.

Her hair in a towel, she got back into bed and reached for the science fiction book she had bought to read on the plane. It was the only thing she had, to kill some time. She didn't want to take one last sentimental walk around the town, she didn't want to see any one, she didn't even want to think. All she really wanted was to get on that plane and get on with starting her new life. She had been filled with hope about starting a new life eight years ago; now she seemed merely to be filled with regret. She knew that nothing that waited for her in New York would in any way make up for what she was leaving behind.

Time seemed to be moving at a different speed that morning, but finally it was time to get dressed and leave. Toby packed, putting the purse with the money at the bottom of the tote bag and packing a pair of jeans, a couple of T-shirts, one pair of sneakers and some underwear on top of it. She put her airline ticket and comb in the side pocket.

She had no full length mirror to see how she looked all dressed up in the suit, but from what she could see of herself by looking down, she seemed to look all right. She thought she ought to look all right after all the money she spent.

She could hear people stirring in the rooms on either side of hers when she opened the door for the last time and looked outside to see if anyone was around. She went out, closed the door behind her but didn't lock it, and silently walked down the length of the porch and then down the stairs. She regretted not being able to say good-bye to Jay, but knew if she even attempted it, she was likely to break down and cry. Someday, if all seemed safe, she might try writing him a letter.

She walked over to Duval and caught a taxi to the airport.

Just the fact that she was at the airport and soon to be taking off, started giving her a feeling of security. She had outsmarted him, and she was thinking with a feeling of exaltation, when, like one of her worst nightmares, she entered the lounge and saw Mac get out of one of the chairs and stare in her direction.

Without pausing to even think, Toby nearly ran to the ladies' room she had just passed and hid in one of the cubicles. How could he possibly have known? Had he seen her go into the travel agency, then checked to see where she bought a ticket to? Did he show up at the airport to monitor all flights out? In fact, had he been following her every movement ever since his arrival?

He must have already known last night when they'd been having dinner together. He must have been laughing up his sleeve the entire time. She thought she was being so smart, and all the while he had been the one who was outsmarting her.

Tears of frustration ran down her face, and she grabbed a handful of toilet paper and tried to staunch their flow. She wasn't a crier; hadn't really cried in years, but she felt trapped now. Caught. Defeated.

She was tired of either giving in to existing conditions or running away. Where was her fighting spirit? Why not just confront the reality and try to change it? Except she felt so alone. Whom did she really have to turn to except a fourteen-year-old boy who didn't need that kind of an added burden? She'd have to do it alone, just as she'd always done everything alone.

One thing was for sure. If she had to confront her husband again, he'd find that the innocent young woman he'd turned into the passive submissive wife was long gone. Toby had a feeling she wouldn't even appeal to him anymore. Added to that, she had now lain in the arms of another man, and that was something he'd never tolerate. That the man had been his paid employee made it all the more ironic. It had been a long time, perhaps he didn't even want her anymore. Except if that was the case, why had he sent Mac to find her? Pride, she supposed. Pride and an almost psychotic need to have her for himself.

When she finally left the ladies' room the airport was virtually empty, and she saw no sign of Mac. No reason for him to stick around, though; preventing her from making her flight had already been accomplished.

She got a taxi outside and told the driver to take her to the Holiday Inn. She'd never been there before, didn't even know that area very well, but it was the kind of place where she wouldn't see anyone she knew.

She explained to the desk clerk that she had missed her flight and would only be staying the night, then signed the register with a name she thought up on the spot. Unless Mac had spies everywhere, he wouldn't find her there.

The room was pure luxury after what she'd been used to. A real bathtub, something she hadn't used in years; a large color TV; even a telephone, although she had no one to call. She took off her suit and hung it up, then got dressed in her jeans before calling down to room service for a late breakfast. There was a pool outside, but she didn't want to be that visible. Instead, she turned on the TV, a novelty after eight years, and settled down on the bed to watch some tennis matches.

She watched tennis with her breakfast, "Wide World of Sports" during dinner, and in the evening watched a series of sit-coms that seemed to bear no relation to real life. By the time the eleven o'clock news came on, her eyes were so tired from watching television that she turned off the set and got ready for bed.

She was afraid that thoughts of tomorrow would keep her awake, but she fell asleep as soon as she'd turned off the bedside lamp.

The next morning Toby checked out of the hotel at ten and asked the taxi driver to take her to the police station. She knew where it was, the island being small, but had managed to steer clear of it for eight years.

When she entered the building she half expected to see her picture on a WANTED poster on the wall. She was nervous; more nervous than she thought she'd be. She had avoided contact with the police for so long she had come to think of them as the enemy.

A young man behind a desk asked if he could help her.

"Do you have a police chief?"

"Yes, ma'am."

"I'd like to see him."

It didn't seem to be as easy as that. "Could you tell me what it's about?"

"No."

The young man seemed slightly flustered. This was a small police force, though, and she imagined they were more friendly than most.

He picked up the phone and pushed a buzzer, then held a whispered conversation with someone before turning back to her and saying, "The Chief will see you. Go down that corridor all the way to the end and you'll see his name, Chief Monroe, on the door."

The office was filled with sunlight, and she saw the view of palm trees and flowering shrubs outside before she was able to focus on the occupant's face. When she did, she got a pleasant surprise. He looked like a younger version of Robert Redford.

"I'm Jim Monroe," he said to her, getting to his feet. "What can I do for you?"—Robert Redford with a southern accent.

She held out her hand to him. "This is difficult, Mr. Monroe."

He waved her to a chair. "Call me Jim. We're pretty informal around here."

She sat down and set the tote bag beside her chair. "I—I'm not sure...."

He ran his hands through thick blond hair. "Listen, would you like a cup of coffee?"

She nodded, glad of the diversion. She wished now she had prepared what she was going to say. Well, she had several things she could say and she'd start with the first. If that didn't work....

He yelled down the hall for some coffee, then arranged a lined pad of paper in front of him and a pencil. "First of all, could you tell me your name?"

"Leslie. Leslie Carrington. Mrs. Howard Carrington." How strange to be using her real name again. It sounded phony to her as she said it.

Her hands were folded in her lap, and she saw him glance at her ring finger. At the same time she glanced at his. Also empty, which proved about as much as hers did.

Two mugs of coffee were brought in and set on the desk, and she reached for hers gratefully. One swallow and she no longer felt grateful.

Jim noticed her expression. "I don't know, I think it must be the coffee machine. We've all tried, and it never turns out decent."

Toby felt herself begin to relax. He seemed very nice. He was also the most attractive man she'd ever seen on the island, but then she'd always been attracted to blondes.

"Look," she finally said, "I've broken the law. I thought maybe you could lock me up." She had thought this over carefully and come to the conclusion that she'd prefer being locked up for life to being forced to return to her husband.

"What'd you do, Mrs. Carrington, jaywalk?"

Her eyes met his own which looked amused. "For one thing, I haven't filed an income tax return for eight years."

He looked a little less amused. "That's the Feds. I suggest you report it to the local IRS office."

"It's not a crime?"

"Sure it's a crime, it's just not in our jurisdiction."

"All right then, I've operated a fishing boat for eight years without a license."

"I think you've been worrying unnecessarily, Mrs. Carrington. You can be fined for that, but we're not going to lock you up."

"What do I need to do to be locked up?"

He leaned back in his chair, his hands clasped behind his neck. "Why do you feel the need to be locked up? If it's guilt over not paying your taxes, the Feds might be able to oblige you."

She looked past him out the window. In the distance, she could see seagulls circling low. "I can't go home, Mr. Monroe; someone's after me."

"Are you saying you need police protection?"

She nodded.

"You want to tell me about it?"

"It's a long story."

He reached for his cup of coffee and finished it off. "I have all the time in the world; we're not exactly having a crime wave down here. But will you call me Jim?"

"If you'll call me Toby."

"Your name is Leslie, but you want to be called Toby?" He was beginning to look at her like he had a nut case on his hands.

"I've been called that for the past eight years. Leslie sounds strange to me now."

"I'm beginning to feel like I'm in one of those detective novels where the mysterious woman walks into the office...." He stopped, noticing that she wasn't amused. "Okay, just tell me about it, in your own words."

"I left my husband eight years ago. Ran away. I was living in California at the time and I ended up in Key West."

"Leaving your husband's no crime, Toby."

"I know that, but to him it would be. He threatened to kill me if I ever tried again. I believe he's capable of it."

"You had run away before?"

She nodded. "Twice. Both times he caught me and brought me back."

"And didn't kill you."

"No, he didn't kill me. Merely humiliated me and increased my dosage of tranquilizers."

He looked like he was beginning to take her seriously. She had often wondered how her story would sound to a stranger; now she was finding out.

"There are divorce courts for this kind of thing."

"He would never have allowed it to get to court. I knew too much about him. About his business. I don't think I'm a fanciful person, Jim, but I truly believe he'd kill me before he'd allow me to go to court, and especially before he'd allow me to come into contact with other men."

"He was jealous?"

"It was a sickness with him. And his temper matched his jealousy." She had to stop speaking for a moment. She had begun picturing Howard in her mind, and the image was doing bad things to her stomach.

Jim reached across the desk and finished off her coffee. "You said you knew too much about him, Toby. Was he into something illegal?"

"Not when we were first married. At that time he was producing movies for TV, and as far as I know he continued to do so. But then he got into another kind of movies. I don't think it was for the money, either; I think it was strictly pleasure on his part."

"Are you talking about porno films?"

She nodded.

"That's not against the law, you know."

"The kind he produced were. He'd go down to Mexico to shoot them. He used children." He had forced her to sit through one of them one night shortly before she left. It was the kind of experience she hoped she'd never have to go through again.

"You couldn't use that as a weapon?"

"I was afraid to use it as a weapon. I couldn't prove anything anyway. I saw one, I knew what he was doing, but it would have been my word against his. And he had some powerful friends and an entire law firm on his payroll."

Jim was looking angry. "If you want to start divorce proceedings in Florida, Toby, I think we could offer you the protection you'd need."

"I don't know."

"Look, for all you know he might have divorced you by now. Have you ever thought about that?"

"I've thought about it, but I have no way of knowing. And I just don't think he would've. Anyway, I know he's still looking for me. He sent a private detective to Key West to find me; he's here now."

He seemed to be coming to some kind of decision. "Look, I'll tell you what you can do for me now." He pushed the pad and pencil over to her side of the desk. "Write down his name, his last known place of residence, where he worked, any telephone numbers you remember, the works. I'll contact the PD out there and have them get onto it. If there are any missing person reports out on you we should find out soon."

She found she could even remember his telephone number at work, and wrote down all the information he asked for. When she finished, he took it out of the office and returned a few minutes later.

"We should have something for you soon."

"Maybe you should just question the private detective."

"Are you sure that's what he is?" *Or are you just paranoid, lady,* he seemed to be saying.

"I know this must sound like some kind of a soap opera to you."

He grinned. "Yeah, but I love soap operas."

"He's got a phony-sounding name, lives on a big yacht conveniently moored next to mine, with, I might add, no visible means of support, and he searched my boat."

"What does he call himself?"

"Mac."

Jim leaned forward across the desk. "About six foot, dark hair, wears fancy clothes?"

Toby's mouth dropped open. "You know him?"

Jim slammed his palm against his forehead. "Damn—you're Mac's Toby!"

Toby slid down in her chair. "You know him, he works with you. I never had a chance, did I?"

Jim was shaking his head. "Something's screwy

here, but I don't know what. I could swear you're telling the truth—"

"I *am* telling the truth!"

"But I know Mac's credentials are good."

"I never said he wasn't a real private detective."

"No, you don't understand. He's with the DEA, and he'll probably have my head for telling you this."

Toby was totally confused. "What's the DEA?"

"Hell, if I've messed up his bust."

"What's the DEA?"

"You really don't know?"

She shook her head in confusion.

"The Drug Enforcement Agency."

"You must be mistaken, or else we're talking about two different people."

"You're the one on Captain Tobias's boat?"

She nodded.

"Then we're talking about the same Mac. I gotta tell you, he figures you for a drug smuggler."

Toby sat in stunned silence for a moment. "I don't know how to convince you of this, but I'd never smuggle drugs. Other things aside, I'd never do anything that might bring me in contact with the police. I've been avoiding the police for eight years."

"Well, I know you don't have any kind of record because we checked out your prints."

"From the Crest?"

He nodded. "Not that that proves anything."

"Why would he think I was a drug smuggler?"

"Mostly because you didn't seem to exist. No records of you anywhere. Hell, we didn't even have a last name for you. I don't suppose you have any ID?"

She shook her head. "None at all. But there are people in California who can prove who I am."

"Yeah, the people you're trying to avoid."

It was hard to believe that all the time she had thought he was a detective, he had thought she was a criminal. "I don't understand. Does this mean anyone without a background is considered a drug smuggler by the government? This just doesn't make sense to me."

"I've blown it anyway, I may as well tell you the rest. A big shipment is expected in Key West, and they figure a fishing boat is going to make the pickup. The other captains checked out—you didn't."

"I know who it is."

"What?"

"I know who your smuggler is. I think just about everyone knows."

"Then why didn't you report it to the police?"

"Because I've been *avoiding* the police! I wouldn't even have reported a crime against *me* to the police. I've been hiding out, don't you understand? I didn't deliberately cheat the government, you know. I would have paid my taxes if I could've figured out a way the information couldn't get back to my husband."

"Well, if you tell Mac, I'm sure that will put you in the clear with him."

"I'm not telling Mac anything."

Her determination seemed to get through to him. "Well that's a crime, you know—withholding information."

"Lock me up."

"Look, this is between you and Mac. He's not a bad guy, though, you know?"

She knew only too well what kind of a guy he was. She found his reasons for having sex with her just as despicable as a government agent as she had as a detective. Either way he had used her, and the fact that she'd also used him was irrelevant. She'd been fighting for her life while he'd merely been doing his job.

Jim picked up the phone and began talking. "Listen, find Mac, will you, and bring him in here. How do I know where he is? Try his boat. He's visible, just look for the best-dressed dude in town. Yeah. Stat, okay?"

"I don't want to talk to him."

"You're going to have to talk to him. Look, I believe you, but these government types... Hey, would you like a burger or something? Pizza? I could send out for it while we wait."

"Sure. Anything."

He smiled at her. "Glad to see you're not too upset to eat."

"I'm not upset at all—just angry at this point. And if he isn't a private detective, then at least my husband still doesn't have a clue where I am."

"Not unless he has friends in the LAPD."

She felt a sinking sensation in her stomach. "He probably has lots of friends in the LAPD."

"Look, we'll protect you."

"Well, if you don't, I can always confess to being a drug smuggler and get locked up." The whole thing was taking on overtones of a farce, and she started to laugh.

"Yeah, it does have its humorous aspects," said Jim. He picked up the phone and she listened as he ordered a pizza and two coffees.

"If you don't want coffee we have a Coke machine in the hall."

"Coffee's fine," she told him.

They were finishing the last of the pizza when Mac, in ordinary faded jeans and a Miami Dolphin T-shirt—the kind of clothes regular people wore—walked in. He did a double take when he saw Toby, a triple take when he noticed how she was dressed.

"What's the story?" he asked Jim.

Jim was looking a bit uncomfortable. "I'm afraid I blew your cover with her, Mac."

Mac pulled up a straight-backed chair, and using the back for the front, sat down. Without even glancing at his watch, he lit a Lucky. "Did you say what I think you said?"

"I said what you think I said."

"Do you have any more pizza?"

"No."

"It's just not my day, is it?" Mac asked, glancing over at Toby again and then away.

"Mrs. Carrington has an interesting story to tell."

Toby almost laughed when Mac said, "Who?"

"Uh, Toby here."

Mac glanced at her again. "I'll just bet she did. I figured she knew I was on to her when I caught her searching my boat."

Jim looked at Toby. She was beginning to feel like the odd member out of a comedy trio. "I was trying to get evidence that he worked for my husband."

Mac's tone was incredulous. "Your *what?*"

"Mrs. Carrington has a husband in California," Jim interspersed. "She thought he'd hired you to find her."

Mac was having none of that. "Of all the simple-minded stories—"

"I believe her, Mac."

Mac looked to Toby. "What happened to Michigan?" he asked sarcastically.

Toby ignored him.

Jim seemed to sense the undercurrents in the room. "Look, Mac, it seems to add up. What did you have on her, anyway? Just the fact that you could find nothing on her. The fact of the matter is, she's been living underground, so to speak, for the past eight years."

Mac muttered a few choice but unprintable words. "Just give a few minutes alone with her, Chief."

"Mac!"

"This is my case and I'd like to talk to her in private."

"Read her her rights, Mac."

"I don't need my rights read," said Toby. "I have nothing to say to him."

With a wary look at Mac, Jim left the office and closed the door behind him. Mac shifted his chair so that he was facing Toby. "What's the rest of your latest alias?" he asked her.

"My name's Leslie."

"You look more like a Leslie."

Toby kept silent.

"Look, Leslie, Toby—whatever. I was going to

level with you anyway. I've got a proposition for you if you care to hear it."

Toby looked out the window. Strange, at the moment she felt no physical attraction for him at all. She hoped that would turn out to be a permanent condition.

"I've been authorized to turn you."

Turn her? What was he talking about?

"What I'm saying, Toby, is that you'll be put on the agency payroll. You've got the connections, you're blown anyway, and we figured you might be willing to work with us."

She gave him a look of astonishment. "You mean be one of your spies?" She made *spy* sound like a dirty word.

"I wouldn't exactly call it being a spy."

"What would you call it?"

"An undercover agent."

"You're crazy—I hate spies! I've been living in fear of spies for the past eight years!"

"Yeah, but now you'd be on the right side of the law."

"I never thought of myself as being on the wrong side."

He stood up and looked down at her, which clearly gave him the advantage. She countered it by looking out the window again and counting the palm trees.

"If I said you'd be doing your country a service...?"

"Forget it!"

"I figured you to be the adventurous type."

"You figured wrong, McQuade."

"Actually it's McTaggert."

"*Ian* McTaggert?"

Now it was he who looked away. "Alastair," he muttered.

Toby had a crazy urge to laugh.

She saw Mac reaching for her container of coffee and quickly snatched it up before he could take it. "You're wasting your time, McTaggert."

Mac seemed about to reply when there was a knock on the door and Jim came back in. "I've got something for you, Toby."

She hoped it was more coffee.

He came around the desk and sat down again, looking very official for the first time. "Your husband's dead."

"She doesn't have any husband," Mac was saying. "That's just some story she'd been feeding you."

"Her story checks out."

Toby was feeling a sense of euphoria steal over her. She had heard the words, and they were just beginning to penetrate. "Dead? Are you sure?"

Jim nodded. "Killed in a pile-up on the San Diego Freeway three years ago. You okay? You want anything?"

A smile of pure happiness broke out on Toby's face. "Okay? I've never been better."

Mac was giving her a look of disgust. "I'm sure glad *I'm* not married to you. Why don't you just run out and celebrate?"

Jim gave him a warning look. "You don't know the circumstances, Mac."

"Three years?" Toby was saying. "You mean I've

been free for three years and never even knew it?"
Three unnecessarily wasted years that she'd never be
able to recover. Three years of unwarranted suspicions and living the life of a virtual recluse when, if
she'd only known, she'd actually been free. For a moment she wondered what her reaction to Mac would
have been if their encounter hadn't been based on
misunderstandings and lies.

"They tried to find you," Jim was telling her.
"What I'd suggest is you get hold of a lawyer. What
with community property in California you're entitled
to at least half of his estate."

"I don't want it."

"I can understand how you feel, Toby, but *all* his
money didn't come from . . . well, unsavory sources."

Mac looked at her with interest. "You have something against money from unsavory sources? What do
you consider the money you get from smuggling?"

Jim sighed. "I think you're off-base on this, Mac. If
you look at it in the light of what we know now, I tend
to believe her that the last thing she would become
involved with was something illegal."

Mac sat down. "It's got to be her. Listen, I'm not
taking her in. I just made her an offer to work for us."

Jim looked from Mac to Toby. "Didn't she tell
you?"

"Tell me what?"

"She knows who the smuggler is."

"You bet she does!"

Jim shrugged. "That's what she said, anyway."

"It's no big secret," said Toby. "Even Rico could
have told you."

"Yeah? Just who are you putting the finger on?"

Toby gave him a disdainful look. "I'm not putting the finger on anyone. It's your job—you find him."

Mac gave Jim a look of entreaty. "I already told her about withholding evidence."

"What did she say."

Toby was getting tired of being talked about as though she weren't present. "I told him to lock me up."

"Look, Toby," said Mac.

"You can call me Leslie."

He ignored her. "Look, Toby—if you tell us who you suspect, and if it checks out, it'll get you off the hook."

She shrugged. "I don't feel I'm *on* the hook. *I* don't do any smuggling. Anyway, where's your proof, Mac? You find some drugs in my toothpaste?" She gave him what she considered to be a brilliant Crest smile.

He was furious. "You just don't care that cocaine's being brought into Key West?"

She shook her head slowly, still smiling.

"I don't get you!"

"Listen, Mac, you want to hear what I think about cocaine?"

"Yeah, I'd like to hear that." Except she was pretty sure he wasn't going to want to hear what she was about to say.

"I just can't get that excited about it, Mac, that's all. It's not like heroin, or even marijuana, for that matter; I mean, little kids aren't becoming addicted to it, and no one's OD'ing on it. It's merely the rich jaded set that goes for it, and if they don't care what they stick up their noses, why should I? And furthermore," she said when she saw he was about to interrupt, "*I* don't smuggle it in, *I* don't deal it—I don't even *use* it. I'm an innocent party in this, despite what you might have thought about me." She paused, a little breathless, surprised that she'd made what amounted to a speech.

"Did your husband ever use it?" Mac shot at her.

"Everyone in Hollywood did coke."

"Even you?"

"No. My husband liked me tranquil, not high."

Jim cleared his throat. "It occurs to me, Mac, that you're beginning to harass one of the citizens of Key West I'm sworn to protect."

Toby smiled sweetly at Jim. "Does that mean I'm free to go?"

He spread his arms expansively. "Free as the wind. Will you be staying on here?"

"Oh, yes."

He cleared his throat again. "Maybe, now that you're free.... Maybe we could get together sometime."

"I'd like that," she told him, aware of Mac's reaction out of the corner of her eye. Well, what did he think, that she was going to continue to see *him*?

"Good," said Jim, looking pleased. "Is there somewhere you can be reached?"

"I have a room at the MerlInn on Simonton."

"Is that where you're going now?"

She stood up and reached for her tote bag. "No. Right now I'm going to go to a bar and celebrate. Thanks to you, this is the best I've felt in eight long years!"

Chapter Ten

"You're just going to let her walk out like that?" Mac couldn't believe that all his plans were just disintegrating before his eyes.

"I don't have anything on her, Mac. Maybe the IRS does, but that's their worry, not mine."

"You really believe that story of hers?"

"It checks out. Anyway, she's not my idea of a drug smuggler. Nice lady; I liked her."

"Yeah, I could see that."

"Does it bother you that I'd like to see her?"

"Hell, no, why should that bother me?" You just didn't mention to some guy who wanted to date the woman you were interested in that you'd spent the previous two days in the sack with her. You also didn't strangle him, but he sure as hell felt like it.

"What are you going to do now?"

"If you hadn't interrupted, I would have gotten the information out of her."

"Not in my police station!"

"I'm not talking about force." What did he think he was, anyway? He'd never do anything to hurt

Toby. Leslie. No, she'd probably always be Toby to him. "She told me she was from Michigan."

"Where did you tell her you were from?"

"Miami."

"Didn't lie to her at all?"

"Hell, yes, I lied to her. It was part of the job."

"And she had equally good reasons for lying to you."

"This still isn't getting me anywhere. The shipment's arriving tomorrow night and I'm back to zero."

"Who's this Rico she said could tell you?"

"Some kid she's got working for her."

"So ask him?"

"I don't even know where to find him. How many kids do you suppose are on the island who're named Rico?"

"Maybe dozens."

"That's what I mean."

"I don't really see the problem, Mac. Not many of the captains do any night fishing, just watch and see who goes out tomorrow night and follow him."

"I'm not exactly invisible."

"You've got radar, don't you?"

"Yeah."

"Do I have to do the job for you? Look, at least you've got an unsuspecting suspect this time. You've been concentrating all your attention on Toby; so whoever it really is doesn't have a clue you're even around."

"You got a point there, chief."

"Anyway, if you spoke to her nicely she might tell you."

"She wouldn't know the truth if she tripped over it."

"You really let her get to you, don't you? Try being nice to her—take her out to dinner."

"I already tried that."

Jim laughed. "Well, Mac, as they say—it's your problem."

The dumb part of it was, Mac was getting really furious at a man he truly liked and respected. He got to his feet and shoved his hands in his pockets.

Jim looked him over. "A Dolphin fan, huh? I had money on the Redskins."

"Figures," mumbled Mac as he left the office.

He found her at the sixth bar he tried, and at each he'd had a sampling of what they had to offer. She didn't look all that lucid herself, leaning over the bar and flirting outrageously with the young bartender who was looking like he'd found the pot of gold at the end of the rainbow.

He cast a shadow over the bar that made Toby look up. "Hey, McTaggert, come to join the party?"

"I don't have anything to celebrate."

"We're celebrating my freedom."

'Hell, I thought you were free before."

"But I wasn't, and now I am. Can I buy you a drink?"

"I buy my own drinks."

"Don't pull some macho act on me, Mac. Remember? I'm the one who threw your camera in the water."

"You're right. I'll have a drink."

The bartender wasn't at all thrilled at his arrival, but

he went off and returned with a beer for Mac. He'd been dying for one ever since leaving the police station.

Mac sat down on a barstool and lit a cigarette. "Listen, Toby, I was hoping you'd reconsidered."

"Reconsidered what?"

He looked to see if anyone was listening, but the bartender was serving someone a few seats down. "You know. With the, uh, gig."

Toby giggled. Yes, she was certainly enjoying her drinks. "No way."

He figured she'd say something like that. "Then how about this? You let me use your boat and I—"

"Forget it, Mac."

"You didn't even let me finish. It would look normal for another fishing boat to be out, but my boat would stick out like a sore thumb."

"You should have thought of that before."

"Does that mean no?"

"That means no."

Toby had always been stubborn, but now she seemed to be getting more stubborn by the drink. He gave a big sigh, almost begging her for sympathy. "Then how about this. Tell me how I can find Rico—"

"I don't want you involving a child."

"Who's involving? I just want to ask him a few questions."

"Forget it. Find your own stool pigeons."

She had probaby been the kind of child who never told on another kid in class. Hell, he'd been that kind of child, too. This was different, though. Drug smuggling was a little more serious than who stole the blackboard eraser. He wondered if the kids who stole blackboard erasers ended up as smugglers when they grew up.

"For a woman of thirty-five you're certainly displaying an irresponsible attitude."

"Thirty-three."

"What?"

"I'm actually thirty-three. I lied."

That was a new one. A woman lying about her age upward instead of downward.

"I didn't think you looked thirty-five." No harm in buttering her up a little.

"I was hoping I didn't look thirty-three."

"You do." On the other hand, no sense in going overboard.

"You want to know something, Toby?"

"Probably not."

"When you saw me at the airport yesterday I was on my way to Miami to see my boss."

"Yeah? Well, you ruined all my plans. I was on my way to New York, but I figured you were following me."

"What were you going to do in New York?"

"Get lost in the crowd."

"New York's a great city."

"Spare me the travelogue, Mac; I'm sure not going there if I don't have to."

"Anyway, as I was saying, Toby, I was going to Miami to see my boss to ask to be taken off the job."

"Why? Didn't the Crest offer up enough clues for you?"

She sure had a mouth on her, this one. Not as loud

as Maria, but twice as sarcastic. Who was he kidding, though? He liked a woman who could dish it out.

"I told him I wanted off the case because I'd become personally involved with the suspect."

Toby leaned over and put her arm around his shoulders. "Oh, Mac, that was so sweet of you." All the time, though, he knew she was laughing at him.

"So why won't you help me?"

"Forget it!"

"Just think of it, Toby—we'd be working together."

"Being a *spy*? I'd feel—sleazy!"

"Are you calling me sleazy?"

"I'm calling your profession sleazy."

"Jim's a cop, is he sleazy?"

Toby considered this for a moment. "Actually he seems like a basically decent guy."

"And I'm not?"

"I'd say you were basically devious and conniving, Mac."

"I didn't get the impression you thought that in bed." A low blow, but she deserved it.

"I generally don't do my best thinking in bed." She put some money down on the bar and jumped off the stool. "Time to hit the next bar. You coming, Mac?"

"What's the matter with this bar?"

"I've already celebrated here. Now I want to go to Sloppy Joe's."

"Spreading the cheer around, huh?"

"You got it!"

Sloppy Joe's was nearly deserted and the bartender looked pleased to see them.

"Two beers, Hank," said Toby, and the bartender

stayed at their end of the bar after he'd served them.

"How's it going, Toby?" Hank asked her.

"Hank, you just wouldn't believe how well it's going. How's it going with you?"

"Well, you could always improve things."

"When?"

"When what?"

"I'm calling your bluff, Hank. When are we going out?"

The bartender looked slightly stunned. "You feeling okay, Toby?"

"Never better."

"Why the sudden change of heart?"

"Because I'm free. I just found out I'm no longer married."

"Yeah? That calls for a celebration."

"That's what I'm doing. So tell me, when are we going to get together?"

"I'm off Sundays."

Mac couldn't believe this conversation was taking place in front of him.

"I have a great idea, Hank. I won't work that day and we can go out on my boat. Swim, do a little diving, what do you say?"

"You're on," Hank told her with a grin, and Mac, feeling worse by the minute, now noticed in the dimness of the bar that Hank was a damn fine looking guy. A little muscular, maybe, probably one of those weight lifters, but a lot of women went for that.

Mac excused himself to go to the men's room, and when he came back Toby was talking to two other guys, but they left upon his return.

When no one was within earshot, he said to her, "What the hell's the matter with you? You're flirting with every guy you see."

"Yeah, isn't it great?"

"What's so great about it?"

"Listen, Mac, if you hadn't been able to flirt for eight years. . . ."

"I don't think you've overlooked one guy."

"Good. Let me know if I do."

Mac was beginning to feel like getting very drunk. "Come to think of it, you never did flirt."

"No. What we did could not be considered flirting."

"Yeah, I guess we went way beyond that." A smile appeared on his face at the memory.

"That's not what I meant. I meant it was all a charade, both of us lying, neither of us meaning what we said. It was a big, fat joke, Mac. An act. None of it meant a thing."

"Is that how you saw it?"

"Sure. How did you see it?"

He was hoping that didn't require an answer. From hopeful dreams of their being together, he was now beginning to wonder if he'd ever see her again. She certainly seemed to have cooled off toward him.

"Come on, Mac—drink up. I want to hit Rick's."

"That's a college hangout."

She gave him a mischievous smile. "Yeah, but those kids are cute."

With a groan he finished his beer and followed her out of the bar. Being the early part of the afternoon, though, Rick's was also practically empty.

He watched while Toby ordered them two more
beers and flirted a little with the bartender. Mac found
himself lighting a cigarette when he already had one
going. Looking around to see if anyone noticed, he
quickly put the old one out.

"You really been faithful to your husband all these
years?"

"I wouldn't exactly call it being faithful. The first
couple of years I wasn't interested in sex, and after
that I was afraid of getting too close to someone."

"You mean like with me?"

"We're not close, Mac."

"What do you mean we're not close?"

"In order to be close to someone the relationship
has to be based on truth. With us it was all lies."

"Yeah, it was, wasn't it. But not anymore. Now we
know all about each other."

"I don't know anything about you except that instead of being one kind of spy you turn out to be
another."

"I feel like I know you, Toby."

"All you know about me is my body. There's more
to me than that, you know."

He thought it politic to change the subject. "Speaking of your body, that's a nice looking suit you're
wearing."

"Thanks. My getaway clothes."

"I can't help noticing your hair's all one color,
too."

"If you hadn't stopped me from getting my flight
yesterday, I'd be a brunette by now."

"Yeah?" He liked brunettes. He tried to picture her

as one but wasn't successful. "Why don't you try it anyway?"

"Forget it."

"I like brunettes."

"Well, I like blondes."

Unfortunately for him the police chief was a blonde. He was sure she hadn't failed to notice that.

"Listen, Toby, could you do me a favor?"

"Don't start on that again."

"No, I was just wondering if we could get something to eat. I haven't had anything to eat today, and these drinks are starting to get to me."

"Mexican food okay?"

It was okay with him, but his stomach probably wouldn't agree. "Anything."

This time Mac managed to pay for the drinks first, then they were out on the street again.

"Incidentally, Mac, I like your new clothes."

"These are old clothes."

"That's what I like about them. Were those other clothes part of your cover?"

He nodded. "I was supposed to look like a rich playboy type."

"You succeeded."

"Then how did you get on to me?"

"You didn't talk like a writer."

"How does a writer talk?"

"About himself. Anyway, stealing my toothpaste was what really did it. It was kind of a coincidence being robbed for the first time just when a new boat appeared conveniently docked next to mine."

She turned into a Mexican restaurant and he followed. He knew Cuban food but wasn't familiar with Mexican, so he just ordered the same things she did. When the food arrived, he didn't recognize a thing. Toby, much to his surprise, was even flirting with the Mexican waiter, and the guy had to be sixty years old.

"I don't believe it. You planning on hopping into bed with every guy on the island?"

She gave him a sunny smile. "No sex. Not until I've seen a shrink."

"A shrink?"

"Yeah, I think I have a problem."

As far as he was concerned, her problem was her suddenly revived interest in men. As far as the sex with her went, he wouldn't remember any problem at all. In fact, quite the contrary.

"What kind of problem?"

"I want to find out why I was the way I was with you."

She had been great with him. And why did some shrink have to hear about it?

"What are you talking about? You were great with me."

"Yeah, too great. I don't think that's normal, Mac. I think it's probably a holdover from my husband."

No wonder the guy had been looking for her. If he had a woman that great, he wouldn't let her go, either.

"What'd he do to you, anyway?"

"You wouldn't want to hear." Okay for a shrink to hear, though.

"I honestly didn't see any problem, Toby."

"Come on, Mac—I acted crazy."

"Yeah." He could remember acting pretty crazy himself.

"You don't think that's a problem?"

He grinned at her. "Look, why don't we go back to my boat and see if we can't solve that problem of yours?"

"Forget it."

He figured she'd say that.

He finished the last of the food on his plate. His head was feeling better, but his stomach was a different matter. He ordered black coffee and hoped it would help.

"You seem so different today, Toby."

"That's because you're seeing me happy for the first time."

"Come on, weren't you happy with me? Not at all?"

She seemed to be trying to remember. Well, he'd revive that memory for her.

"There was an instant attraction, Toby, you know it. And we were perfect together—absolutely perfect."

Her face softened. "It was good, Mac, but it wasn't real."

"Then what the hell is real?"

"I'm hoping a shrink will help me find out."

"*I'll* help you find out. I just don't believe it wasn't mutual. I'd almost go so far as to say it was love at first sight."

She smiled. "Almost, huh?"

"Yeah, almost." He was damned if he was going to

declare his love in a Mexican restaurant. If it even was love, although he was beginning to suspect that was the case. He knew one thing for sure: he didn't want all those other guys on the island getting their hands on her.

"Listen, Mac—I was swept off my feet by a man once, and I've spent the last eight years hiding from him. I just don't trust that kind of emotion anymore."

"I know where you're coming from; I was married twice."

"No, you really don't know where I'm coming from."

"Want to sail off into the sunset with me? Maybe a little island off the coast of Belize?"

She smiled. "My boat or yours?"

"Hell, the government owns my boat."

"Don't rush me, Mac. I'm just getting used to being free again."

"All I'd have to do is just reach over and touch you. That's all, just one touch—"

Her lips became soft. "I know."

"You're feeling it, too?"

"Yeah, I'm feeling it. But I'm not going to do anything about it."

"You know something? I broke it off with my girlfriend Maria yesterday."

"Because of me?"

"Partly. As it turned out, it was mutual."

"So you're free now, too. We both have something to celebrate."

"Do you think we might work something out together?"

"I don't know, Mac. Let me try to get my life together, first."

"I know I've been moving in on you too fast. It's something about this place, like everyone's on a perpetual vacation, you know what I mean?"

"That's part of its charm."

"Yeah, but it's like you're on this week's vacation and if you don't score fast.... Sorry, that wording left a lot to be desired. I think it's still the drinks talking."

Toby was nodding. "I know what you're talking about. It all happened so fast, and we never even got to know each other."

"Do you want to get to know me?"

She nodded. "Of course we're not exactly neighbors."

"Miami's not that far away."

"Let's just not rush anything, Mac. You go back to Miami, I'll stay here and get my life in order. We'll see how we feel with some distance between us."

"There was some distance between us yesterday, and I never stopped thinking about you."

"Yesterday was too soon to tell."

What she was saying made a lot of sense. How did he know for sure it just wasn't some infatuation, anyway? Maybe a couple of weeks away from her and he'd forget what she looked like. He had a feeling he wouldn't, though, and his intuitions were usually correct. It wouldn't hurt for her to go out with other men. Hell, if it turned out she preferred one of them to him, then what they had wasn't worth beans anyway. Better to find out now than later.

"You sure you aren't that smuggler?"

Toby's eyes took on a gleam. "You'll just have to watch my boat and find out, won't you?"

Mac laughed. "Well, you always were a pretty good liar."

"Want to hear about my childhood in Michigan?"

"Where are you really from, California?"

She nodded. "Born and bred."

"How does it compare with Florida?"

"If you mean Key West, no comparison. I haven't seen the rest of the state."

"Key West's all right for a weekend, maybe. Any longer than that and I think it'd get boring."

"I don't find it boring."

"It's a small town; I'm used to cities, I guess."

"I think it's perfect."

"Well, nobody's forcing you to leave it."

"Nobody could force me to leave it. Not anymore."

Her tone had turned cool, and he had the feeling he should have brought a halt to the conversation when he was ahead. He picked up the bill before she could confiscate it and put down a tip. "Come on, I'll walk you back to your boat. I just remembered I'm down here on a job, and now I've got to start again from scratch. Unless, of course...."

She shook her head as she stood up. "Don't ask me to do that, Mac. The charter boat captains are a pretty close knit group, and the man you have in mind is well liked. I have to live here—I'm not getting involved with this."

"And you also don't think there's anything wrong with cocaine."

Her eyes darkened. "I wouldn't use it; I just can't get overly concerned about the kind of people who do."

"And no little speech on patriotism would change your mind?"

"My sense of patriotism has never been directed toward the tax system, Mac. And it seems to me that's the bottom line on drug smuggling."

"You've got a point, Toby, and some of the things you've said I agree with. But it's not the users I'm after. It's the ones raking in billions every year, most of them foreigners, and all of them ripping off the country. They think they're above the law, and I just happen to disagree with them."

Toby was looking thoughtful. "Okay, Mac, and I don't entirely disagree with you, either. I guess I just hadn't thought that much about it. But it's still your job, not mine. And I'm not going to help you. And you can tell your boss that being a spy isn't my idea of a lot of fun. It's going to be so great being able to be out in the open, I never want to have to lie or be devious about anything again."

They walked out into the sunshine, and Toby paused on the sidewalk. "I'm not going back to the boat just yet, Mac. I want to stop by MerlInn. Every cent I have in the world is in the bottom of this tote bag, and I want to get it back in the safe."

He leaned down and kissed her on the tip of the nose. He'd wanted to do that since they met, and wondered why he hadn't done it sooner. Just the quiet stuff was nice with her, too; it didn't all have to be passion.

"See you later then, Toby."

"See you later, Mac." She turned and walked away from him and he waited for a minute to see if she'd look back, maybe wave, but she never turned around once. But that was okay; he knew he'd be seeing her again.

Mac couldn't get over the change in Toby. He could lose her, he knew, if he wasn't careful, and that was something new for him. He was usually the one who told women to get lost. Well, maybe not that crudely, but none of them seemed to hold his interest for very long.

She was so different from any of the women he had known. But the things that he admired about her could be just the things that would cause trouble between them if they ever did get together. Her strong independence for one, and the fact that she didn't depend on others for help. He liked little things about her. The fact that she wasn't preoccupied with how she looked to the exclusion of everything else. Preoccupied? She didn't even seem interested. She seemed perfectly happy to wear cut-off jeans and a T-shirt and to hell with fashion. If more women felt like her, the retail business would be in deep trouble.

He saw her love for Key West as the most difficult obstacle he'd have to overcome. Sure the place was cute, quaint was probably the right word, but all it really was was a tourist trap, and the tourists seemed to be either gay or college-age. He had nothing personally against either, but they just weren't the kind of people with whom he'd develop friendships. And nothing ever seemed to happen in Key West. He'd never been a fishing enthusiast, and there were just so many bars and restaurants you could hit in one day. God knows Miami had its problems, but there was also an excitement to the place, the feeling you could come across something every day that you hadn't seen or experienced before. Even if his work didn't keep him there he'd never head for some resort town and spend the rest of his life being bored to death.

Not that he thought he'd find Toby boring, but there was more to life than just a woman, and in his case more meant his work. It probably would have worked out better if he had been a travel writer. Too late to change professions now, though, and besides he had trouble just writing the reports required in his profession.

Yeah, there were drawbacks to the whole thing, but he still wanted Toby, and he'd do his best to get her. Let her taste her freedom for a while; he was sure she wouldn't soon forget what they'd had going for them. He knew he wouldn't.

The hell with it all—he'd worry about it later. Right now he had a job to do, and he no longer had a clue how he was going to go about doing it. In Miami he had any help he needed at hand; here it was just him against them, and for the first time in his career he began to question his own capabilities.

As it turned out, he almost got a commendation for doing practically nothing.

Mac had watched on Tuesday night as one lone fishing boat set out at about nine. He was still watching five hours later when the boat steered into Garrison Bight. The other boats in the marina seemed to be unoccupied as he waited in the shadows of the dock and watched as the man, Captain Warren according to the sign fronting the slip, dropped anchor and prepared to leave the boat.

It was all so ridiculously easy it wasn't even fun. Mac flashed his ID at the man, made sure his gun was visible, and Captain Warren almost literally fell apart. He let himself be taken into custody without a struggle, and was more than happy to tell Mac his contact in the Bahamas and how the pick ups were made. The cache itself was impressive and he could have found it himself in minutes, only the good captain was so eager to point it out he didn't have to.

Mac's only regret was that Toby wasn't there to see his triumph, but then she might not have viewed it that way. He took the morning flight out to Miami, Captain Warren in tow, and acted extremely nonchalant when George congratulated him on a difficult job well done.

Later the contact in the Bahamas was picked up and he turned out to be equally cooperative. They were given the name of the source in Colombia, which information they passed on to the Colombian authorities, who in turn would be bought off as usual and soon their business would return to normal. All of which was frustrating, but then real life usually is.

Mac was offered a couple of weeks off, but he said no, feeling he'd rather just keep working. With Maria gone the condo was as dead as a mortuary, and it was too soon to pay Toby a visit. He would give her a little time as she requested, but then—watch out, Toby, because there'd be no stopping him.

Chapter Eleven

Toby felt that the perpetual smile on her face was no doubt stretching it out of shape, but her happiness was such she wanted to share it with the world. Her natural friendliness was at last allowed to surface, and now that she was open to it, she seemed to make new friends every day.

There was Jackie, the saleswoman at Peaches, where she'd gone to replace her ragged bikini and ended up staying to share the woman's lunch. Toby rarely went to movies because she hated to go alone, but now she had a friend who shared that feeling, and they ended up seeing movies together most Friday nights.

One of the first things she had done was send to California for her birth certificate, and when it arrived she borrowed Jay's car in order to get a Florida driver's license. She didn't plan on getting a car as it was scarcely needed on the small island, but it was the kind of identification she had long needed. This also enabled her to get a library card, where she met her second friend. One of the librarians was just her age, also single, and turned out to be a scuba buff. Often, when Toby had no clients, the two of them would take off on the *Free Spirit* and spend long hours exploring the coral reefs. And with her reading matter no longer restricted by her fears and paranoia, Toby was back to reading mysteries and sometimes caught herself thinking that her own life had been more interesting than the books. Not that she had any desire to relive those years.

She began dating with frequency, but quite honestly the thrill of that began to wear off after a few weeks. She found that despite prostestations to the contrary, men weren't really satisfied with a platonic relationship, and she didn't feel ready yet to start anything else. Not that she probably couldn't have been persuaded if the conditions had been right, but even with Jim, whom she'd grown very fond of, and who made her laugh with stories of the sort of inept criminals that occasionally frequented the island, she felt no stirrings within, not even when he kissed her goodnight. Toby found herself wishing it could have been different with him. He was exactly the sort of man she should be attracted to. He had the kind of looks she liked, he was decent, intelligent, humorous, and he loved Key West quite as much as she did. But the chemistry wasn't right, and no amount of wishful thinking could make it otherwise.

One of her first orders of business had been to see a lawyer. On the matter of her back taxes, he advised her to see an accountant and recommended several to her. He said if she found herself in legal difficulties with the IRS he'd help her out, but he didn't think that was going to be the case. He also put forth a very good argument for her using her share of her late husband's estate to pay any back taxes that might be due.

"Just figure that he owed it to you, Toby. If you hadn't felt forced to run away from him you never would have had this problem. Further, any divorce court in California would have awarded you half the community property."

But Toby was adamant on this point. She wanted nothing having to do with her husband, especially his money, intruding on the new life she had built up for herself. And it had been *his* money. He'd had most of it at the time they were married.

It turned out that Toby had so many expenses and write-offs connected to her charter boat business that the accountant jokingly said that the government might end up owing her money. As it turned out, her back taxes came to several hundred dollars, but Toby had the money to cover it and she breathed a sigh of relief at once more being a tax-paying citizen.

She put it off for a while, but finally one day she asked Jay if he knew a shrink on the island that he could recommend.

"For *you*?" he asked her in astonishment.

Toby nodded.

"You'd be the last person I'd expect to need a shrink. You're the most together person I know."

"Not quite as together as I seem," she told him.

He did know of one, a man who specialized in helping homosexuals, but it turned out he wasn't gay himself, and since he usually helped the men with their sexual problems, Toby thought he would suit her fine.

It was with some trepidation that she went to her

first session with Dr. Shaefer, but his off-beat form of professionalism soon put her at ease.

He had the requisite beard and wire-framed glasses, but he also had a penchant for painting seagulls, and large oils of the birds were hung all over his office. In addition to that, he played background music during the sessions that sounded like waves breaking upon the shore. What could have been humorous, instead turned out to be a lulling atmosphere, and she soon felt perfectly at home there.

He thankfully wasn't one of those psychiatrists who wanted to delve deeply into all aspects of her childhood. Toby's childhood had been both happy and uneventful, and only the death of her parents in a Las Vegas hotel when she'd been a senior in college had been at all traumatic. They had died in a tragic fire that had taken the lives of many, and the tragedy had been in the newspapers and on television for days. And yet, she felt her parents, who had been inveterate weekend gamblers, would have probably viewed it as a fitting way to go. And at least they had gone together, not a small thing for a couple that close.

Instead Dr. Shaefer asked her what the problem was, and Toby told him it had to do with sex. In this case she thought background was important, so she began to tell him something of her life with her husband.

"What we have here is the classic dominant/submissive relationship," he said when she'd sketchily outlined the details. "And yet you hardly strike me as the submissive type."

"I don't think I am. I don't think I was even at the

time. But I'd always been attracted to strong men, and he was perhaps the strongest I'd ever met.''

"And charming, I imagine."

"Extremely charming. He was older, successful, and in addition, I found him very sexy. And I was innocent sexually at that point, which was rare for a California girl in college, believe me.''

"Was there some particular reason for this innocence?''

"It wasn't a matter of morals. I mean I wasn't adverse to sex, didn't look on it as a sin or anything. I think it was more a matter of the boys I dated backing off too easily. I wanted one of them to take control, and they always seemed to leave the control to me.''

"What you needed was a man who was stronger than you were.''

"Exactly. And none of them were.''

"And what about this man? The one you married? Did you have sex with him before your marriage?''

Toby nodded. "Actually I think that's what precipitated the marriage. Before that I think he found me intriguing, but that was mostly because, being a producer, he always had actresses pursuing him furiously, and I never acted like that. I was so surprised he wanted to see me at all that I never would have thought to take the initiative myself.''

"What happened when you first had sex with him?''

"Well, he was totally dominant, of course, and being inexperienced and rather shy at my first contact with a man's body, I left it all up to him and hardly even participated. For some reason this really turned him on. But what was important was that he hadn't thought I was a virgin, and when he got proof that I was, he immediately wanted to marry me. He said I was a rarity; that this was his chance to form me into what he'd always wanted in a woman."

"And is that what he did?"

"I suppose it was. But I think it was also the cause of his becoming almost pathologically jealous. He was the only man who had ever made love to me, and he wanted it to remain that way. I'm sure I wouldn't have been unfaithful in any case, but he took steps after our marriage to insure I couldn't, even if I had wanted to."

"What kind of steps?"

"Before we were married he took me to a lot of Hollywood parties. The men there would sometimes make a fuss over me, more because of my lack of sophistication than anything else, I think, but after we were married he no longer wanted me along at those parties. And if for some reason I did go, he'd make me dress in loose clothes—quite unbecoming clothes—and if another man so much as talked to me, he was capable of going into a jealous rage and accuse us both of making an assignation behind his back. It was the same wherever we went. If waiters seemed to be overly polite to me at restaurants, he would accuse me of leading them on, and often drag me out of the place before the food arrived."

"But what of your life, your married life I'm referring to now, when your husband was at work? Did you also work?"

"He would never have allowed me to work."

"Just a happy housewife?"

"I wasn't even allowed to be that. He had a full staff of servants, and the only thing I had to do for myself was get dressed in the morning. My husband didn't even like me to go out shopping alone, and if I really had to, the chauffeur went along. On matters of clothes, my husband wanted to go along and pick them out for me. He said I had no taste, and I guess I didn't have much being right out of college where all I'd worn were jeans."

"And he dressed you in those unbecoming clothes?"

"That was only for when we were out in public. At home, it was one of two different modes of dress. He either liked the Fredericks of Hollywood look—dressing to look like a stripper—or he liked me to look like an innocent little girl."

"How did he manage that?"

"Oh, a number of ways. It could be with my hair in braids, wearing a frilly little white dress, white cotton anklets—that kind of thing. If he could've married a child, he probably would have."

"But a child couldn't have worn the stripper look successfully."

"You're right. I guess he liked the combination. In either kind of dress, though, I was supposed to act submissive at all times, to treat him as the master."

"What kind of problems did you have with this?"

"None at first. The first year it was a gradual thing, and I was very much in love with him. It was like playing games, and I didn't mind that. And I also had nothing to compare it with."

"And after the first year?"

"As I said, it was a gradual thing. But I began to tire
of it after awhile, particularly the restrictions on my
activities. I'd always been on the go in college, played
a lot of tennis, had a lot of friends. But when the honeymoon was finally over, I began to be bored to death.
I still liked being alone with my husband, but the days
alone seemed interminable. When I found myself
watching daytime game shows, I finally confronted
my husband and told him I was beginning to climb the
walls. He insisted I see his doctor, and that man put
me on tranquilizers. After awhile I was walking
around so doped up by the tranquilizers that I don't
even remember what I did with my days."

"And what about the nights? Did you enjoy the sex
with him?"

"He insisted that I always remain passive during
the sex. I was to do no contributing of my own, just
merely be the recipient of his actions."

"And how did you feel about this?"

"I became conditioned to it, I guess. The passive
part, I mean. I really wasn't sure sex wasn't always
like that, anyway. I admit to loving the sex. After
awhile it was the only thing I loved about my life.
Even when I no longer loved him, he had the ability
to make me forget everything else. At least for a
time."

"Did you ever try to leave your husband?"

"Twice unsuccessfully, and then the last time when
I ended up in Key West."

"Do you want to tell me about it?"

"There was one friend I had had all through school,
Marianne. She worked days and nights and weekends.

I was constantly with my husband, so I never got to see her. But sometimes she'd call me during the day, and one day I started telling her about my life and I found she was getting very upset. She told me I should leave him, get out of there, but I wasn't quite ready for that yet. But one day I was, and that day she took off from work and drove by the house to pick me up. Only the chauffeur had taken down the number of her license plate. The next day my husband found me and forced me to go home."

"Were there any reprisals on his part?"

"Several. First he punished me as though I were a child. No television, no sweets—practically everything but standing me in a corner. That was also when he started threatening—and I believed him—that he'd kill me if I ever left him again."

"Do you think he was capable of that?"

"I think he was capable of anything."

"And the second time?"

"The second time I didn't even get off the property before the chauffeur had brought me back and called my husband at work. And the servants, who before that had taken orders from me—although I seldom gave them—now assumed authority over me."

"But he didn't kill you."

"No. But I think I convinced him that I'd only been going for a walk. And after that the dosage of tranquilizers was increased."

"And the third time was successful?"

Toby nodded. "But I planned it a little better that time. First, I stopped taking the tranquilizers about a month beforehand. I think I had some kind of withdrawal symptoms at first because I didn't feel very well for about a week, but after that I seemed to grow stronger every day."

"Didn't your husband notice?"

"Never. I acted the same way I had acted when tranquilized. And that time when I left, I made sure the servants were elsewhere. The chauffeur was out on an errand, and the rest of the staff was occupied with their work. And maybe luck was with me, too, because I got away with it."

She told him about her flight, about meeting John, and about her subsequent life in Key West, only leaving out the part about Mac.

"That's a frightening story you've told me, Toby, but I honestly fail to see the problem. You seem perfectly healthy and adjusted to me, remarkably so in light of what you went through. You just got on with making a new life for yourself and succeeded admirably."

"Well, there's this man."

"A new man?"

She nodded. "I met him a few weeks ago." She went on to tell the doctor about how she'd thought Mac was a detective sent by her husband, while all the while he'd suspected her of being the drug smuggler he was out to catch.

"So this man was actually the catalyst that enabled you to be free at last."

She hadn't thought about it that way before.

"So is there some problem with this man? Does he perhaps remind you of your husband?"

"In ways."

"You want to tell me about it?"

She wasn't actually sure she did. But that's what she was paying him for, wasn't it?

"Well, he's strong. And probably capable of jealousy."

"We're all capable of jealousy, Toby. It's the degree and how we handle it that counts."

"I guess it was my reaction to him more than anything."

"You mean your suspicions?"

"No. I mean my physical reaction."

"Are you saying it was strong?"

"Very strong."

"And this was after an eight years' abstinence?"

She nodded.

"I'd say that's also perfectly normal. After all, sex was the one thing you enjoyed throughout your marriage."

"I just don't think my reaction to him was normal. I wanted him almost instantly, Doctor. It was as though he bewitched me."

"And that seems bad to you?"

"Somehow this is more embarrassing to tell you than the story about my husband."

"That's only because it's more immediate."

"The thing is, all this man has to do is touch me and I practically dissolve on the spot. At first when we had sex I was passive, like I had always been, but then he asked me to touch him, to do what I wanted, and I'm afraid I went rather wild."

"You mean you hurt him?"

"No. Nothing like that. I just think my responses

were somewhat... wild. I seemed to lose control of myself while we were having sex.''

"Was he a good lover?"

"Fantastic! At least I thought so. And I felt so—so free being able to respond however I wanted."

"I think you're wasting your money, Toby."

"What?"

"I'm beginning to feel I'm taking your money under false pretenses. I think it probably did you a lot of good to tell me about your marriage, but confiding in anyone would no doubt have helped. But this new relationship of yours—I've got to say it sounds ideal to me. There ought to be more women around like you."

"You don't think I get too carried away?"

"Doesn't he get carried away?"

"I suppose so. But I don't like the feeling of losing control, Doctor. I don't like the feeling I could become as addicted to this man as I was to my husband."

"Toby, not all men are like your husband. In fact, not many of them are, thank God. And as far as this man goes, you're in control of your life now, aren't you?"

She nodded.

"And you're also in control of whether you see him or not."

"I'm not so sure. I really want to see him again. I've been going out with other men, but I just don't feel the same about them. The magic isn't there."

"You know what it sounds like to me, Toby?"

"What?"

"It sounds to me like you're in love. You always lose control in love, don't you know that? And there's always some dependence on the other person, even if it's only emotional. He's probably feeling much the same way you are. And if you lose a little of that hard-won freedom of yours, you'll be gaining a great deal of happiness in return. Don't be afraid to give your love again, Toby. If you do that, then I think your late husband will have had his revenge."

"I don't think it's love I'm afraid of."

"Marriage?"

She nodded. "I don't mind giving up a little of my freedom, I suppose, but I'm afraid in marriage I'd have to give up a great deal."

"Only if you want to. Personally, I think you could handle it very well. I don't see you ever giving up all of what you've gained for yourself. You worked too hard to get it."

The doctor stood up and held out his hand. "The best of luck to you, Toby. I don't think you'll need to be seeing me anymore."

"Not even if I need someone to talk to?"

He smiled. "Try talking to your man. I think he's going to turn out to be very understanding."

Toby headed back to MerlInn feeling ten pounds lighter. On the way back she stopped at the hairdresser's and did away with her bangs and shoulder-length hair in favor of a new, shorter cut that waved back from her face and made her eyes appear larger. Taken with her new look, she stopped at Fast Buck's and treated herself to some new T-shirts. Unlike her plain white ones, these were colorfully striped. Now that she didn't need runaway money, she found she had a healthy balance in her new bank account and felt she could afford to spend a little on herself. And some of it was earmarked for fixing up her boat.

It had been six weeks since she had last seen Mac and she found she missed him dreadfully. Short of calling the DEA, though, she didn't know how to reach him. It could be that he no longer wanted to see her, but she wouldn't know that unless she made some attempt to find out.

Toby finally decided that when she got back to MerlInn she would write him a letter in care of his agency. A letter was something else she hadn't done in years, and she found herself looking forward to it.

As it turned out, it wasn't necessary. As though reading her mind, there were three messages for her that Mac had called, and she was to telephone him at a number in Miami.

She'd wanted some time and he'd given her some time. But, damn it, wasn't six weeks long enough? Any longer and she was liable to forget him. As it was, he was having trouble picturing her in his mind. He could remember other things about her quite well, though.

Work had been keeping him busy, thank God, but then there was never a shortage of work for the DEA in Miami. There was never a hiatus in the drug business.

When he wasn't working, though, his life seemed in no kind of order at all. There were women he could call, but he didn't. The idea of any woman other than

Toby did nothing for him at all. He played racquetball occasionally with colleagues, but his mind was never fully on the game. He put more time into his work than was necessary, in an attempt to forget her, at least momentarily, but even that wasn't successful. He wanted to see her, and he wasn't going to be put off any longer.

The day came when he returned to his condo early and could no longer suppress the desire to get in touch with her. If she wanted to see him, great. That's all he asked. If she didn't want to see him, then at least he might be able to get on with his own life. As it was, he felt suspended in a kind of limbo. And thus the messages left at the MerlInn.

When she called him back there was a quality to her voice he hadn't heard before. Not as ebullient, perhaps, as the last time he had seen her, but filled with a happiness that for some reason made him uneasy. He selfishly wanted her happiness to come from him rather than outside forces.

"So how're you doing, Mac?" she asked him.

"Great. Working hard. How about yourself?"

"I find I thrive on starting over."

"Keeping yourself busy?" *I read that to mean you have been seeing other men, Toby*, but he kept that thought to himself.

"Very busy. There doesn't seem to be enough hours in the day. And I'm meeting so many people. People who have been here all along, but it took me eight years to become friendly."

"I miss you, Toby." To hell with chit-chat, he wanted to get down to basics.

There was a pause, then, "I miss you, too."

"You really mean that?"

"I have no reason to lie to you anymore."

"Great. When are we going to get together?"

"Whenever you come down."

"How about coming up to Miami for the weekend?"

"Why Miami?"

"Because I happen to live here. I've seen where you live, I figured you could check out my abode."

Another pause, and he began to think she'd say no. But she surprised him. "All right, I'll get the flight out on Saturday."

"Will you stay at my place, or should I get you a hotel reservation?"

No pause at all this time. "Your place will do fine."

He terminated the conversation pretty quickly after that, not wanting to give her a chance to change her mind. Anyway, talking to her on the phone was no substitute for seeing her in person.

When he met her at the airport she was wearing the suit he'd last seen her in, but the red and white striped T-shirt beneath was new. As was the way she was wearing her hair. He decided he liked it. It looked fluffy and soft and framed her face in a becoming way.

Mac took her straight to a restaurant in Bal Harbour for lunch and saw that she was taking in the scenery on the way. The drive from the airport didn't happen to be scenic, but he thought he could show her parts of Miami that she'd like. There wasn't any real conversation in the car, just some polite talk to fill in the empty spaces. He hadn't been nervous before, but now he began to feel like he was out on his first date and trying desperately to impress the girl.

Conversation while they were ordering lunch seemed strained, too, so he ordered a bottle of champagne.

"What's the occasion?" she asked him, looking every bit as good as all the well-dressed women surrounding them. Not that she didn't always look good to him.

"No occasion. Well, hell, Toby, it is our reunion."

But she was smiling as though sensing his nervousness. "Don't apologize—I love champagne. And I think I need a little loosening up."

"You nervous, too?"

"Not about you; I'm just not crazy about flying. Give me a boat any time."

Mac, who preferred airplanes to boats, didn't say anything.

They both had steak sandwiches, and Mac felt as responsible for the food as though he'd prepared it himself. It turned out to be good, though, so he had one less worry.

"You sure you don't mind staying at my place?"

"Why should I mind?"

"Well there's only one bed, and the couch isn't the kind for sleeping."

"My shrink said—"

"I don't want to hear about your shrink. Lot of nonsense, all that stuff."

"I fully intended having sex with you when I said I'd come up. Of course if you—"

"Me? Listen, I'm glad to hear that."

"That did seem the one thing we were compatible about."

"Oh, come on, Toby—we're compatible in lots of ways."

"Name one."

He thought about the things he liked to do, and then he thought about the things she liked to do. For some reason none of them seemed to coincide.

"We both like champagne," he finally offered, and even that wasn't the truth. He didn't like champagne much at all, it had just seemed like the right gesture at the time he'd ordered it.

She laughed for the first time. "Well, then, if we spend our time together drinking in bed we won't have any problem."

Mac spent the rest of their time at lunch telling her about the wrap-up on the Key West investigation, and if she found it boring she didn't say so. In fact, she asked some good questions, but not once did she congratulate him on his work. Of course, she, more than most, knew how little work he had actually done.

When they were finished he asked her if she'd like to look at the shops. There was a Saks and a Neiman Marcus and all kinds of other stores not available to her in Key West. He thought she'd be impressed by the new plaza.

"What for?" Toby asked.

"Don't you like shopping?"

"No, do you?"

"Well, we've got that in common, at least. Although I was looking forward to showing you the Polo Shop."

Again she laughed. "Spare me. And I'm glad to see you're dressing more normally these days."

"You don't look quite right out of your shorts and T-shirt."

"Don't worry, I brought them with me."

He figured they'd spent enough time observing the amenities. What he really wanted was to get her back to his place and see if the chemistry was still there. As far as he was concerned it was. Just sitting across from her was getting him pretty hot and bothered. The thing was, he couldn't discern the same reaction in her.

She gave his living room only a cursory look as he led her inside. Well, what did she expect? Pictures on the wall? Hanging wall plants? He didn't go in for that kind of nonsense.

Mac started to ask her if she wanted a drink, but then she was moving toward him, so instead he took her in his arms and kissed her the way he'd been wanting to kiss her for hours—and it was still there, all the old magic. She started to tremble the minute he put his hand up under her T-shirt to feel her bare breast, and after that they were getting out of their respective clothes as though in a race with time.

It was as good as ever. It was better than ever. It was better than he'd ever thought possible. Their bodies seemed to know each other in ways their minds were still trying to deal with, and when they were finished he had no doubts about her at all. She was perfect as far as he was concerned, and if he couldn't have her, then he doubted he'd ever be satisfied with another woman.

Tell her you love her, you idiot, was going through his mind, but before the words could actually form themselves, she said, "My shrink told me—"

"Spare me the psychological hyperbole, Toby." The last thing he needed to know was her shrink's opinion of him, which would no doubt not be complimentary.

She moved her head from where it had been resting on his chest and looked up at him. Her hair was mussed up and there were red marks on her chin from where his rough chin had irritated her, but he thought she had never looked more beautiful.

"You don't like psychology?" Toby was asking.

"Nope, nor shrinks, either. Bunch of garbage." Mac had had to go through psychological testing in order to get his job, and the series of tests had struck him as nonsense. *Do you ever feel suicidal when you get up in the morning?* Really, like anyone with an ounce of intelligence would answer yes to a question like that and expect to get a job. He had lied, of course. When he had a championship hangover he often felt suicidal in the morning. Didn't everyone?

"Oh. Well, he told me I'm in love with you." She said it all in a rush like she was afraid he'd interrupt again.

Mac was stunned. "He said that?"

She nodded, averting her eyes.

"Well, some shrinks have their heads screwed on right, I guess. He really said that?"

"Yes."

"Is it true?"

"I think so."

"Well, what are we going to do about it? I mean, it goes without saying that I feel the same way."

"It doesn't go without saying, Mac," she said with a warning in her voice.

"You mean you want me to say it?"

"Only if it's true."

"Oh, it's true all right."

"Then say it!"

Well if together in bed wasn't the right time, when was? "I love you, Toby."

"I love you, too."

They took a moment out of their conversation to kiss, then he said, "Well, what are we going to do about it?"

"I don't know. I'm not about to live in Miami."

"You haven't even seen it yet."

"I've seen enough."

"Well, I'm not about to quit my job. What did you have in mind, me taking over Rico's job?"

Toby shook her head.

Stalemate.

The rest of the weekend had its ups and downs, most of the ups taking place in bed. The downs were all the highlights of Miami that she didn't seem to appreciate. He thought one of the selling points would be his season tickets to the Dolphin games, but it turned out she didn't even like football. He had thought everyone from California liked football.

In fact, the only place she seemed taken with at all was the sleazy bar where he met Boogie. The man had some information for him and she wanted to be taken along, and he was already apologizing for the place before she even saw it. But she liked it—said it had character—and even got a kick out of Boogie, who was on his best behavior in front of Mac's new woman.

Mac hated having to take Toby back to the airport Sunday evening, but they both had work the next day. He insisted on buying her a present at the airport store. She didn't want perfume, didn't want candy, and finally relented and let him buy her a beach towel with seagulls printed on it. Not his idea of a romantic gift at all.

He was sure he'd feel bereft when he watched her plane take off, that he'd be useless until he saw her again the following weekend when it was agreed he'd come to Key West. But instead he drove back home in a state of euphoria that lasted several days. Just knowing he was going to see her again kept his spirits up, plus he would call her at the MerlInn several times during the week.

Work fouled up his plans to visit her the following weekend, though, and it was two weeks before he finally got down to Key West. This time she had borrowed Jay's car and met him at the airport.

Mac found that just seeing her, though, wasn't enough. She hadn't cancelled her charter boat fishing, and he had a choice of either going out with them and doing some fishing, or staying in town by himself. Something had to give.

He broke it to her when she drove him back to the airport on Sunday. "This can't go on, Toby."

"What can't go on?"

"I want to see more of you than this. Hell, I don't even *like* fishing."

"Look, Mac, since you cancelled out last weekend I wasn't sure you'd really come this time, otherwise I could have cancelled the fishing parties. Next time I will, okay?"

"Can you afford to do that?"

"I'm making more money than I need. Anyway, I'd rather be able to see you."

"You could see me all the time if you lived in Miami."

"I can't do that, Mac."

After that, things were better. It was as though he had two vacations a month, and Key West wasn't a bad place to spend an occasional weekend. They spent days at the beach, nights making love, and the rest of the time eating good food. She even got him interested in scuba diving, and he became as enthralled with it as she. In fact, he found he liked the weekends in Key West better than the ones when she visited him in Miami. Except for one minor detail; the bunk in her boat just did not fit two comfortably. But since she was putting money into fixing up the boat anyway, he persuaded her to add a larger bunk, and she agreed with alacrity.

But while he enjoyed those weekends on the island, he was always glad to be back in Miami. There was something about cities that enervated him in ways small towns could never do.

It was a warm Saturday in October when Mac got around to asking her to marry him. They had spent a

few good hours scuba diving and were now heading
back to port. He brought up two beers from the galley
and handed her one as she steered the boat. He
opened his and leaned back against the wall, watching
her.

"You want to hear something, Toby? That first
time I was alone in here with you, well, I wanted you
so bad it almost made me sick. I mean I actually felt
like I was coming down with the flu or something."

"I felt the same way."

"No kidding?"

"No kidding. I remember thinking that if Rico
hadn't been on board...."

"Yeah. If he hadn't been...."

"It had been so long since I'd felt anything like that
I couldn't understand my feelings at first."

"Oh, I understood mine, all right. And you know
something else, Toby? I still feel the same way. About
wanting you. I don't know, the feeling never goes
away."

"I feel the same way. And I hope the feeling never
does go away."

"Does it make you happy?"

"So happy at times that I'm afraid we're tempting
fate."

"Yeah, I feel the same way." He glanced at his
watch. He was down to one cigarette an hour, but he
didn't want to miss it. Was this the time to ask her, or
should he wait for a more romantic setting? What was
more romantic than here, where he'd first been attracted to her?

"I'd like us to get married, Toby."

She looked over at him. "Is this a proposal?"

"Do I have to get down on my knees?"

"Heaven forbid you should do something that romantic."

"I will if you want."

"Have you thought about this, Mac?"

"Of course I've thought about it. What did you think, it was just a momentary urge?"

She laughed. "I don't know—it could have been lack of oxygen from the diving."

"I'm serious, Toby. Here I'm proposing, and you're making jokes about it."

"Does this mean you're going to move to Key West permanently?"

"No, that's not what it means. I'm not ready to retire."

"I'm not moving to Miami, Mac."

"I didn't figure you would."

"Then why get married? I don't know about you, but I think we have a perfect arrangement."

"I'd just like it legal, that's all. I'd like to know you belong to me."

"I feel like I belong to you now. I'm not seeing anyone else, you know that."

"I'd just be happier if it were legal. It wouldn't change anything, except I'd feel more comfortable. Right now you're my woman or my lover or whatever. I want you to be my wife."

"You've already been married twice. I thought you said never again."

"They say 'three's a charm,'" he said, not believing he was actually using those words.

"Yes, but I'll be on two, and two's not a charm."

"With me it will be."

"All right, if it makes you happy."

"Are you saying yes?"

"I'm saying yes."

"Come here, I want to put my arms around you."

"Wait 'til I dock the boat, Mac, okay?"

"If I have to," he grumbled, but the grumble masked the happiness he was feeling.

That night they broke the news to Jay who immediately responded by giving an impromptu party in their honor.

"When are you going to do it?" he asked them.

Toby looked at Mac. "I figured next weekend," he said, seeing no reason to wait.

But Toby disagreed. "No, next weekend we'll spend in Miami as usual so I can go shopping for a dress. We will get married in Key West, won't we?"

"Anything you like," he assured her.

"You going on a honeymoon?" asked Jay.

Mac looked at Toby. "Why not? I can take some time off. Where would you like to go?"

"How about a cruise?"

Mac felt he got enough of boating on alternative weekends. "How about Europe?"

"You mean fly there?"

He nodded.

"I don't think so. I don't mind flying to Miami anymore, but I don't think I want to fly across an entire ocean."

"What about that island off Belize you talked about?"

Her eyes lit up. "No kidding? We could go there?"

He smiled into her eyes. "Of course we can go there. Why not? I'm kind of getting to like islands."

Toby bought a pale blue linen dress with olive trim, and Mac decided to go with some of the Ralph Lauren clothes that were still hanging new in his closet. They bought each other gold rings shaped like ropes which Toby found appropriate, and Mac, who had refused to wear a wedding ring in both prior marriages, didn't argue at all.

The wedding was held at the MerlInn with Jay playing background music on the piano. Rico, now fifteen and feeling very important, gave Toby away, and the wedding guests included the police chief, and Toby's new friends: her lawyer, her accountant, and her shrink.

There was one little hitch in the ceremony when the judge asked him, "Alastair, do you take this woman, Leslie Robbins, to be your...." and then stopped at the look of astonishment on Mac's face.

"Who?" he seemed to be asking.

The judge looked to Toby. "That's my name, Mac."

"Robbins? I remember the Leslie, but not the Robbins."

"That's my maiden name. My legal name now. At least for the next few seconds, if we can get on with this."

Mac felt a little silly. The judge was probably wondering if he knew whom he was marrying. He nodded his head and the ceremoney continued.

After it was over Jim came up to congratulate him.

"This is quite a surprise," the police chief told him. "Last time I saw you two together you were ready to kill her."

"It's a long story," said Mac.

"I'm sure it is. I'd love to hear it some time."

Instead Mac told him how the case had wound up.

"If you're planning on settling in Key West, we could use you on the force."

"No, I'm staying in Miami."

"Toby's moving to Miami?"

"No, Toby's staying here."

"Sounds ideal," said Jim, but Mac wasn't sure he believed him. So people wouldn't understand, so what? He and Toby were doing what made them happy, so what did it matter what other people thought.

When the time came to leave, Toby's friend from the library drove them to the airport. They were catching a plane to Miami, and then getting a connecting flight to Belize.

Toby insisted on sitting in an aisle seat, and once the plane was airborne she grasped his hand tightly.

"Why are you hanging onto me now? The dangerous part is over," he told her.

"What are you talking about?"

"The take-offs and the landings are the dangerous times, we're fine, now."

She looked disbelieving. "Are you telling me the truth?"

"Of course I'm telling you the truth."

"Well, I wish you hadn't told me. The only parts I enjoy are taking off and landing—now I won't enjoy any of it."

"Sorry you married me?" he asked her.

"Not yet."

"What do you mean, 'not yet'? Are you expecting to be?"

She gave him an impish grin. "You never know."

"Well, I know," Mac said, pulling her into his arms as far as the armrest would allow.

From the way she responded to his kiss, he was sure she knew, too.

Epilogue

"You know something, Toby? I think we got the system beat." It was the middle of December, and Mac was helping her string Christmas lights across the boat for the annual Christmas parade around the island.

She was looking forward to the parade, and had even persuaded Mac, albeit reluctantly, to don a Santa Claus costume for the event.

"What are you talking about, Mac?" Up until then their conversation had revolved around where to have Christmas dinner, and for the life of her she couldn't figure out what system that had anything to do with.

"The system, Toby, the system. I'm talking about our marriage."

"What about our marriage?"

"We managed to beat the system, that's what."

"Could you explain that?"

"What I mean is, we've avoided all the pitfalls that society sets out for married couples."

"You mean like mortgages and babies and community property?"

"To name a few. In most marriages, the man is required to be the breadwinner and the woman is required to be a housewife."

"Not these days, Mac." Although she knew that had been the case in his prior two marriages.

"You're missing my point. The truth of the matter is, our marriage is a continuous weekend vacation for both of us. Hell, you don't even have to do my shirts."

"I wouldn't anyway."

"You wouldn't?"

Toby laughed. "I know what you're talking about, Mac, and I agree. But you know something? If the day ever comes when you retire, we're going to have to learn to live with each other."

"You think we couldn't?"

"I think it would be an adjustment."

"I suppose I'd have to take up fishing."

"You might even get to like it."

"When I do retire, though, I'm not planning on living on this boat. It's okay for weekends, but I like a little more room."

"We could get ourselves one of those conch houses."

"You'd live in a house?"

"I have nothing against houses, Mac."

"You know those books you used to read?"

"You mean the how-to books?"

"Yeah. You could write one yourself. 'How to Have a Weekend Marriage,' or something along those lines. Set it all out for the reader. I bet lots of people would like a marriage like ours."

"No, we just lucked out. I think most married couples live in the same town, and commuting between two places in the same town would be a bit ridiculous."

She finished with her lights and went across the deck and helped Mac finish up with his. If his ability to fasten the lights was any indication, he wouldn't be all that handy around a house. She'd do the Christmas tree herself while he was in Miami.

"Hey, Toby, you want to come down to the cabin while I try on my Santa Claus suit?"

"You've already tried it on for me three times."

"Yeah, well, I think it might need a little adjusting."

She didn't know why she'd ever had the idea he was a good liar. His wish to get out of his clothes was so transparent she almost laughed out loud.

"I don't think it's playing Santa Claus you have in mind, Mac."

"Don't you want to see what Santa has for you?"

"I think I have a good idea what Santa has for me."

"Don't you want it?" His arms were reaching out to pull her against him, and her body was reacting before her mind.

One hand slid up under her sweat shirt and she leaned into him. He could always do it to her, and this time was no exception. "Mac, anyone on the dock could see us."

"I know. I think we ought to go down to the cabin."

"You're going to make a perfect Santa; you never get tired of bestowing your gifts."

"You never get tired of receiving them, do you?"

"Never," she agreed, and then his mouth closed over hers, and the magic between them once again reasserted itself.

Toby had found it didn't take much to make her happy. It only took Mac.

Share the joys and sorrows of real-life love with
Harlequin American Romance!™

GET THIS BOOK FREE as your introduction to Harlequin American Romance – an exciting series of romance novels written especially for the American woman of today.

Mail to:
Harlequin Reader Service

In the U.S.
2504 West Southern Ave.
Tempe, AZ 85282

In Canada
P.O. Box 2800, Postal Station A
5170 Yonge St., Willowdale, Ont. M2N 5T5

YES! I want to be one of the first to discover
Harlequin American Romance. Send me FREE and without obligation *Twice in a Lifetime.* If you do not hear from me after I have examined my FREE book, please send me the 4 new **Harlequin American Romances** each month as soon as they come off the presses. I understand that I will be billed only $2.25 for each book (total $9.00). There are no shipping or handling charges. There is no minimum number of books that I have to purchase. In fact, I may cancel this arrangement at any time. *Twice in a Lifetime* is mine to keep as a FREE gift, even if I do not buy any additional books.

154-BPA-NAXF

Name _____ (please print)

Address _____ Apt. no.

City _____ State/Prov. _____ Zip/Postal Code

Signature (If under 18, parent or guardian must sign.)

This offer is limited to one order per household and not valid to current Harlequin American Romance subscribers. We reserve the right to exercise discretion in granting membership. If price changes are necessary, you will be notified.
Offer expires December 31, 1984.

AMR-SUB-1